LITTSIE OF CINCINNATI

Jinny Powers Berten
Norah Holt

Illustrated by Elizabeth W. Schott

FOUNTAIN SQUARE PUBLISHING LLC: CINCINNATI

Manufactured in the United States of America
Library of Congress Control Number: 2002096372
ISBN 0-9724421-03

Illustrations: Elizabeth W. Schott   www.ewschott-fineart.com
Page design: ElizabethW. Schott
Cover design: Elizabeth W. Schott

Printed in the U.S.A.
First American Edition, 2003

Fountain Square Publishing LLC: Cincinnati

www.fountainsquarepublishing.com

DEDICATION

To members of our families who came from
Ireland to America and changed this country by
their enthusiasm, courage, and self-reliance.

A SPECIAL NOTE OF THANKS

We would like to thank Yeatman Anderson, Charles Issets, Bobbie Kuhn, Lucille Blocsom, Dan Pinger, Carolyn Meeker, Louise Head, Bill Galligan, Charles Neff, Lee Pfalzgraf, Daniel Hurley, Janet Miller, Dottie Lewis, Bonnie Williams and Frank X. Prudent for helping to make this book a reality.

Thank you to Mary Ellen Powers for her time and energy and a special thank you to Francis Forman who, at the time of the writing of this manuscript, was the reference librarian at the Cincinnati Historical Society.

Authors' Note

Although the story of *Littsie of Cincinnati* is fiction, it is based on actual historical events and the lives of people who lived in Columbia and Cincinnati, Ohio, from 1800 to 1850.

CONTENTS

CHAPTER 1 - DISCOVERIES: 3

CHAPTER 2 - A NEW HOME: 9

CHAPTER 3 - THE CAVE: 14

CHAPTER 4 - DOWN RIVER TO CINCINNATI: 19

CHAPTER 5 - A SUDDEN CHANGE OF FORTUNE: 26

CHAPTER 6 - THE SEARCH FOR AID: 32

CHAPTER 7 - THE STRICKEN CABIN: 36

CHAPTER 8 - THE LOST CHILD: 38

CHAPTER 9 - ALONE IN THE FOREST: 42

CHAPTER 10 - THE RESCUE: 45

CHAPTER 11 - THE RETURN TO HEALTH: 51

CHAPTER 12 - AN ANSWER: 55

CHAPTER 13 - THE STRANGER: 66

CHAPTER 14 - ARRIVAL IN NEW ORLEANS: 71

CHAPTER 15 - MY LIFE AS A GOVERNESS: 76

CHAPTER 16 - BACK ON THE RIVER: 82

CHAPTER 17 - A SOLUTION: 89

CHAPTER 18 - MEETING A TRUE FRIEND: 93

CHAPTER 19 - ONLY A SINGLE CLUE: 102

CHAPTER 20 - A FATE DECIDED: 110

LITTSIE OF CINCINNATI

DISCOVERIES

THE snow fell quietly on the hills around Cincinnati. It drifted against doorways, covered the statues that stood in the center of the city in Fountain Square and swirled around the horses and buggies as they rolled along the streets.

It was one of the coldest days in January 1884 and the Ohio River had turned to ice. Earlier in the day some brave people had walked across to the Kentucky shore.

The cold wind blew hard against the little brown house on Liberty Street, rattling the windows and doors. But the fire in the parlor fireplace warmed the room where I sat. My grandchildren, who also lived in the house, ran to see me. It was the quiet time after dinner when I always told them a story.

Come over here, let Grandma Littsie tell you a tale of the times when I was a child, living in the Ohio country." They enjoyed hearing stories about what life was like when I was a little girl. That was way back in the 1830's, over fifty years ago. I'll tell you, those were the days, if you were strong and wiry, like myself, that is.

When did it all begin? Well, let me think. I guess it was that beautiful blue, sunny morning in March of 1832 when just about everything in my life had changed. I remember standing on the deck of our flatboat holding tight to the heavy oar balanced on the stern post. I searched the bank of the Ohio River and the distant hills for signs of Indians.

Now to tell you the truth, I knew there were no Indians. Cousin Shawn, whose farm we lived on in Pittsburgh, told me the Indians moved west twenty-five years before our little boat rounded the river's bend. I was eleven years-old at the time and, as my Mama always said, "a terrible daydreamer." I was all legs and arms. My hair was the same auburn color as my Mama's and wispy too. It was always blowing about my head, I could never keep it in place and, to be honest, I stopped trying.

I imagined what life was like when the Indians were here. As our boat floated along from Pennsylvania into the Ohio country, I whispered the names of their rivers, Monongahela, Muskingum, Allegheny, Kanawha, Scioto, Ohio.

For our journey down river to Columbia, my father put me in charge of steering the flatboat, his way of keeping me out of trouble, or so he liked to tease. My Papa, he was a special man. He had a great generous heart and a smile for everyone.

When I wasn't steering the boat, Mama asked me to take care of my sister, Megan, the worst little redheaded dickens of a four year-old. She was into everything. I couldn't turn my back when she was on deck. She would tease the chickens and the pig we had in a small corral on the front of the boat. Often she would lean far out dragging her hand in the muddy river water, about to

fall overboard at any moment.

At night all four of us slept inside the small cabin in the center of the flatboat. That cabin was something. It was filled from floor to ceiling with all we needed for our new house. There was a spinning wheel, a plow, a grindstone, spades and rakes. Apples and flour, pork and salt were packed tightly in barrels, stacked one on top of the other. Of course, there were the precious spring seeds kept dry in tin boxes, stored on shelves around the top of the cabin.

We were on the river about three days when we saw other travelers like ourselves. You can imagine how excited I was when I saw another flatboat.

"Papa, Mama, there's a boat coming toward us!" I shouted. Both of them rushed out of the cabin and Papa took the boat and guided it closer to shore.

"Hello, we're the O'Donnells, bound for Columbia," Papa shouted.

"We're the Allyns bound for all towns along the Ohio. We are river merchants. See, our calico flag tells you that."

Standing in front of the flag waving from the stern post was a fat little man, with a black beard, who stood about five feet tall. He wore a brown checkered shirt and red plaid baggy pants with yellow suspenders that kept his pants from falling down around his big round belly. A thin woman, wearing a bright red gingham dress, stood at his side.

"We're about to have lunch," Mama called.

"Stop and share our food," Papa added.

"My wife, Emily, and me were thinking of stopping. We'll be happy to join you," the man smiled.

Papa and Mr. Allyn steered their boats toward a small cove, where they tied the lines to some trees. We jumped off the boat on to the muddy riverbank. I helped Mama spread a cloth on the ground between two large logs, a perfect place for our meal. While Mama cut large thick slices of yellow cheese, I gave Mr. and Mrs. Allyn, Papa and Megan some hard crackers and apples.

The Allyns said they were river merchants and knew the towns along the Ohio better than most steamboat captains and so Mama and Papa asked them about Columbia. They told us it was the oldest settlement in the Miami Purchase. Mrs. Allyn said she knew stories of the early days in Columbia that "could raise the hair on your head," as she put it. And the woods were so thick that even someone who knew them well could get lost and never be found.

"Captain Benjamin Stites, one of the first settlers in Columbia, built three block houses in the town where the settlers went to hide from the Indians when they came on a raid. One of the block houses is still standing at the boat landing," Mr. Allyn said. "You'll see it near the riverbank, about a half mile past the mouth of the Little Miami River. It's a good marker. Straight back from there you'll see the town of Columbia. The beautiful city of Cincinnati is just five miles down river from there," he added.

As the Allyns told us about Columbia, Megan wandered away. Mama called to her to come back but the stubborn little monkey only laughed. I ran after her as fast as I could and when I was almost at her side, I tripped over something sticking out of the mud.

I was so angry, I scrambled to my feet, and tugged and pulled at it so I could throw it into the river, but before I did, I gave it a closer look. It was flat and black, with strange writing along the edges. "Look at this!" I called, as Papa and Mr. Allyn ran up the riverbank toward me.

Mr. Allyn took my discovery and examined it carefully saying, "This is wonderful, Littsie. The inscription is in French. Now my French is only fur trader French, but here is what I think it says, 'L'annee de notre seigneur, 1749 . . . the year 1749. 'Et pendant le reigne de Louis XV, Roi de France' . . . in the reign

of Louis the Fifteenth, King of France."
He couldn't make out the rest but the
end of the quotation was clear . . .
"et en commemoration du
retablissement de notre possession' .
. . as a token of renewal of
possession."

  This, he said, was one of the
original markers the French left
along the Ohio river in 1749 to claim
the river for France.

  "But does this mean that France
owns the river? " I asked.

  "Oh no, dear, not any more.
They gave it up to England and then, of
course, you know how America gained independence
from England. "Keep the marker in a safe place, Littsie.
This is a treasure," he smiled, handing it to me.

  "I'll put it on top of the seed tin. Nothing will
happen to it there," I said.

A NEW HOME

EVERY evening after supper, as we headed for Columbia, we sang this song:

> *The boatman is a lucky man,*
> *No one can do as the boatman can,*
> *The boatman dance and the boatman sing,*
> *The boatman is up to everything.*
> *Hi-ho, away we go,*
> *Floating down the river on the O-hi-o.*

First Papa would hum a few notes and then Megan and I would join in with the words. Papa bowed to us as we curtsied to him and the three of us danced a little jig around the deck of our flatboat.

Sometimes Mama walked out of the boat's cabin, drying her hands on her apron saying, "Well, for heaven's sake! Are we having a party? Come now, Littsie and Megan, settle down, it's time for bed."

Megan and I slept inside the cabin on two narrow planks suspended between two apple barrels. Before lying down, we knelt on our bed and looked out the window to see the other riverboats. Sometimes we called out a "hello" to them as they passed. Then we snuggled under the covers, surrounded by the sweet smell of the apples, and went to sleep.

Our last night on the river, I woke up to the loud
blasts of a boat's foghorn. I tiptoed out on the deck. The
fog was so thick I could hardly see the edge of the boat.
The sound of the horn grew louder. There was a rush as
if hundreds of boatmen paddled the water. The fog
cleared and I saw a steamboat moving like a floating red
and white crystal palace. Just before the boat slipped
into the fog again, there was her name, *Virginia*, above
the paddle wheel.

Waves from the passing steamboat rolled one after
another against our boat. It pitched and tossed and I fell
to the deck, almost rolling overboard. Once the water
was calm, I crawled back toward the cabin, as the door
swung open, there was Papa.

"Good heavens, Littsie!" he cried, "what are you doing out here?"

I tried to explain, but he would not listen, saying, "Come inside, child. You should be asleep, not wandering around the deck in this fog."

As I followed him into the cabin Megan cried, "Oh no! Littsie! Look your marker broke in two pieces."

"It must have fallen from the seed tin when the waves hit our boat," I said, taking the broken marker from Megan.

"That's too bad, little one," Papa added.

"Oh, Littsie, may I keep half?" Megan pleaded.

"All right, Megan, but keep it safe," I told her.

The next morning, after the fog cleared, we went on our way down river. In the afternoon, our boat rounded a bend and Papa called out, "There's a blockhouse at a landing just ahead!"

We could see Columbia about a mile from the river in the middle of a flat open plain. The town was surrounded by hills so heavy with trees I just knew wild animals roamed there. We tied our boat at the dock and walked up the muddy road leading to the town.

We pushed open the door of Stites' General Store. The room was filled from floor to ceiling with just about everything a person could imagine.

"Welcome. What would you like to have, ladies and gentleman?" a short gray haired man asked as he stood behind the counter.

Papa said, "Our name is O'Donnell. We've come

down river from Pittsburgh looking to buy farmland. We hear that the land is good in this part of the Ohio country."

"Well, it's true, Mr. O'Donnell. I'm Mr. Athan Stites, the county land agent in these parts. Come, sit, rest in these chairs around the stove," he said. "The land is real fertile. I've seen people take out as many as eighty bushels an acre at harvest time."

"Not in one crop!" Papa exclaimed.

"In one crop," answered Stites.

"Glory be," Mama cried, "In Pennsylvania we were lucky to get thirty bushels."

"And these hills are filled with mighty fine eating. Columbia is fondly called 'Turkey Bottom'. There are hundreds of wild turkeys up there," confided Mr. Stites.

He got up and went behind the counter where he pulled out a metal box. Opening it, Mr. Stites said, "There's a track of land I think would be perfect for you Mr. O'Donnell. Here it is. It's eighty acres, at $1.25 an acre. My horse and wagon are hitched up out back. I'll take you there so you can see it for yourself."

As Mr. Stites drove his wagon from behind the store, a honey colored dog came running, barking playfully at the two black horses. "O'Donnell, is that your dog?" Mr. Stites called out.

"No, I've never seen her before," Papa answered.

"Go on, go home," Mr. Stites shouted at the dog, panting happily beside the wagon. "She won't bother us, once we're on our way," insisted Mr. Stites. The stray followed the wagon, keeping a safe distance from

Mr. Stites' whip. The wagon rolled down the muddy
road past freshly plowed fields.

A few cows in a grassy pasture looked up
indifferently as the wagon rattled over the road. About
a mile from Columbia, we turned off onto a narrow
path.

Mr. Stites said we would walk the rest of the way.
"This Indian path leads into a meadow. Wait, you'll see
how beautiful it is," he said, pushing ahead through the
overgrown branches. As we came to the clearing, Papa
held Mama's hand and said, "You know, Sheila, I feel
we're home." Smiling she replied, "It looks grand to me
too, Michael."

"Well, then, Mr. Stites, we'll buy these acres."

"We'll go back to the store and I'll draw up the
papers this very afternoon. You can take them to
Cincinnati to the land office tomorrow," explained Mr.
Stites.

I was so happy, I ran up a small hill, grabbed a vine
hanging from a tree and swung out as far as I could
yelling, "Whoopee! Whoopee!" The honey colored stray
ran to me wagging her tail and barking. Mama and
Papa said I could bring her with us and I named her
Alana after my grandmother's dog back in Ireland.

THE CAVE

THE next few months Megan and I helped our parents clear the land and build our cabin. First, using the wood from the boat, we built a shelter we lived in while we cleared the land. This was hard work. We had to chop down many trees. Some of them were three, even five feet wide. It took a lot of muscle and a lot of time to cut one down and even more time to cut it up. Those dark, old and powerful trees gave us so much, lumber for the cabin, fences for the animals, furniture, wagons, and wood to keep us warm. The trees we didn't cut down sheltered the turkeys, raccoons, deer and squirrels that gave us many tasty dinners.

When the sides of the log cabin were up, neighbors from the town came to help put on the roof. Oh, my, what an exciting day that was! When I saw that roof go up, I knew I was home, that we would celebrate birthdays and Christmas, the changing seasons, love and laughter, in our own cabin. The neighbors brought lemonade, cakes, watermelon, corn, all kinds of good things to eat. What started as work, ended up a party. That's when I met Tommy and Sally.

Sally was eleven, just my age, and Tommy was a year older. Tommy knew the Little Miami River and the hills around Columbia better than anyone. All that summer of 1832, when we finished our chores, we went on what

Tommy called "exploring expeditions." We searched for wild turkeys and deer and bears in the nearby hills. One hot afternoon in July, as we were exploring, we pushed through hanging vines and found an entrance to a cave.

"Think we should go in?" Sally asked hesitantly.

"Well, I don't know," replied Tommy.

"What if there's a bear inside!" I exclaimed.

"Ain't no bears inside caves in the summertime!" Sally said, as if she knew all there was to know about the whereabouts of bears.

"If it's their den, bears protect it. That's what my Pa says," insisted Tommy.

Then I asked, "What if an awful ferocious animal is inside?"

"Ah, Littsie, come on, let's just go in and have a look," said Tommy. Parting the vines we started into the dark opening to the cave. Suddenly a gruff voice shouted, "I wouldn't go any further."

We looked at one another and ran out of the cave. Stumbling, falling, we got caught in the vines.

"Ah, ha, trapped like three deer! That'll show you to trespass on other people's property," the husky voice called out.

We huddled together, looking toward the voice, high in a tree outside the entrance to the cave. The woman was dressed in a leather skirt and jacket and wore a broad brimmed leather hat. She swung down through the branches of the tree to the ground. Standing before us with her hands on her hips she said,

"Well, explain yourselves."

Tommy stepped forward. "I walked all over these hills, ma'am, and I didn't know anyone lived up here."

"Well, you don't know everything there is to know about these hills, do you?"

She was a fat little woman about five feet tall. Grey hair was sticking out from under her hat. Her face was

tanned and wrinkled and her deep blue eyes flashed with excitement when she spoke.

"All right, tell me your names," she demanded.

"I'm Littsie O'Donnell."

"Speak up, you," she said pointing to Tommy.

"Tommy O'Brien," he said, clearing his throat.

"And you there."

"Sally Totten, ma'am."

"My name is Anne Bell Bailey and this is my home," she smiled, leading us into the cave.

We walked about twenty feet through a quiet, cool tunnel to a large room full of little lanterns. One lantern was on a small round table, another was by her bed. In the center of the room was a fireplace. Anne Bell showed us her "natural chimney," a hole in the ceiling of the cave where the smoke went out. Then she told us to sit on the small bear skin rug on the floor near the fireplace.

"I suppose you're wondering why I live in these woods in a cave. You may think I should be at home like other women my age. Well, that is not the life for me. It once was, but never again. I've seen more than spinning and weaving in my day. I keep this cave so I can get away from the city folk and from my son, William. He's a farmer. He lives in Gallipolis, Ohio, with his wife and two kids. William would be happy to see me settled. But I can't do that! Oh, I do have a house. It's really a hut made of fence rails near the Kanawha River in Virginia. I hunt and fish and have a great time there," she laughed. Standing in the glow of the lantern's light she asked in an English accent, "Would you know I am named after the good Queen Anne of England?"

She stirred the smoldering ashes of the fire with a metal poker. Sitting down again she said, "You see, many years ago I was born in Liverpool, England. I was a fine lady, wearing silk and lace. That was when I first came to America. I lived with my relatives, the Bells, in Staunton, Virginia. There I met my husband. The good, brave and dear man was killed at the Battle of Point Pleasant in Virginia, October 10, 1774. When I heard of his death, I swore revenge. I would never live as the 'grand lady' again, no matter what."

Anne Bell sat down in a small wooden chair and leaning toward us continued, "My friend, Mrs. Moses Mane, gave me a hand raising my infant son, William, so I could join the garrison at Ft. Lee, near Charleston, Virginia, as a frontier scout. I took on missions where I dodged Indian parties and delivered supplies and ammunition to the fort.

"I bet you've seen everything in your lifetime, Miss Bailey," I said, staring at this strange woman.

"Yes, and some so bad I don't care to remember. Like the time I stole some gunpowder, and the lost children I found, and the people I saved on the Wilderness Road. And I know you want to hear about the Indians who were in these parts. But it's near suppertime for me and I'm sure your folks want you younguns to be at home. So be on your way."

"Could we come and visit you again, Miss Bailey?" all of us begged.

"Why, of course," she smiled. "When the white flag is flying outside my cave, you'll know I'm here. Stop in, I'll be glad to see you."

As we headed down the hill, we turned back to see our new friend. She stood with her hands on her hips keeping watch as we went on our way.

From the day we met Anne Bell Bailey, once we finished our chores, we climbed the hill to her cave. Often we took Megan and Sally's sister, Rachel, with us too.

On rainy afternoons Anne Bell invited us into her cave. We sat for hours listening to stories about Indians, of narrow escapes, near drownings and dangerous adventures of the early settlers in the Ohio country. Other days we hiked through the woods with her and she told us all she learned from the Indians.

She would say, "There is plenty to eat in these woods. No need for a body to starve, unless they're too foolish to know what's good for them. Here are some wild onions. Over there are some red crab apples. There is some fine food right here on the banks of the little Miami River."

"Cattails!" we shouted, as Anne Bell handed them to us. "Once they're cooked, they're delicious."

In August, when harvest time came, we had to work in the fields with our parents. We could not go for visits with Anne Bell, but we remembered all she taught us.

4
DOWN RIVER TO CINCINNATI

ON a morning in late September Papa said, "Littsie, this Friday I'm going to Cincinnati. Would you and Tommy like to come with me? Tell him to ask his folks."

Friday was a cool, clear fall day. The sky was a cloudless, bright blue and the river was like glass. Papa guided our rowboat down the Little Miami River into the Ohio.

I closed my eyes and listened to the water slapping at the sides of the boat. The smell of the river in the crisp autumn air reminded me of early spring when we came to Columbia.

As we got closer to Cincinnati, we counted fifteen steamboats tied up at the public landing. We watched men hauling huge barrels of flour, whiskey, pork, bales of cotton and boxes of furniture from the steamboats. Crews, polishing the boats' brass and washing down their decks, waved to us as we passed.

There were no women on the dock, only men, and many of them were black men. "I thought all black people were slaves, Papa. What are these men doing here in Cincinnati?" I asked.

"Ohio is a free state. Just over there," he said, pointing to the banks on the opposite side of the river, "Kentucky allows slavery. When slaves want to escape, if they make it across the Ohio River to Ohio, they have a chance to stay free. But sometimes it doesn't last. Slave catchers are allowed into Ohio to get runaway slaves, so they can be returned to their masters."

"My Pa says, some black folks travel north of Cincinnati so they don't get caught," said Tommy.

"You're right, Tommy. The slave catchers would have a harder time finding them." I watched those black men until Papa told me not to stare. I prayed that the slave catchers wouldn't find them. I couldn't imagine what it would be like to be a slave and not to be free.

The dock was at the foot of a small hill where Papa

steered our rowboat into a space near other small boats. Papa pointed to a street sign saying, "This is Main Street. It leads to the center of town. Since I have business to take care of at the land office, I will trust you to be on your own."

Holding his gold watch he said, "It is almost noon. We'll meet here at 4:00 o'clock. That will give you time to see Cincinnati." Littsie, here is my watch. Keep it in your pocket," he said, handing it to me.

As we walked up the landing, we saw pigs everywhere. They were in the middle of the street, behind shops and in the front yards of beautiful homes. There was even a huge sow nursing five piglets in the doorway of a fine ladies' dress shop. One hog was so bold as to come up to us and sniff at our shoes. Slowly, he waddled away to feast on garbage dumped in the middle of the street.

"Cinicnnati does a big business in pork," said Papa.
"They send pork off to New Orleans, St. Louis and many
other places. No one minds having a pig around because
it puts money in people's pockets. Hogs run wild in this
town. There's enough garbage in the streets for them to
eat, so they won't hurt you, but stay out of their way. The
land office is just ahead, see you at 4:00 o'clock."

We walked down tree lined Fifth Street to an open
market. There was a maze of farmers' tents, carts and
wagons. Behind some of the stalls men and women sat
around cook stoves drinking sassafras tea, smoking their
pipes and talking.

In the market, the pigs shoved their snouts into
rotten apples and cabbages. They growled and pushed
anyone who got in their way of a tasty morsel.

We turned a corner and there, at the end of the
street, was a huge sign that read: "The Great Western
Museum, See the Invisible Girl, the Chamber of
Horrors, the Infernal Regions! All this for fifteen cents!"
Since we only had a dime each for spending money, we
looked down an alley that ran alongside the museum.
We decided to peek into an open window about six feet
from the ground.

I climbed on Tommy's shoulders and when I was
about to see inside, a hog pushed Tommy's legs. He fell
and I tumbled on top of him and the pig.

"Are you hurt, Littsie?" he asked, helping me to my
feet.

"Well, she deserves to be! The very idea! Stand up

girl, when an adult speaks to you."

The woman was short and plump and stared at us through a pair of gold-rimmed spectacles attached to a handle she held in her right hand. She had bright red rouge on her lips and cheeks and her dark brown hair was in tight little curls.

"Frances Trollope is my name and if you have any decent raising you'll tell me yours!" she insisted.

"Littsie O'Donnell and this is my friend, Tommy O'Brien."

"And just what are the two of you doing? Come on, explain yourselves," Mrs. Trollope demanded.

"Well, ma'am, you see, it all looked so wonderful. You know, the 'Invisible Girl' and all. We have only twenty cents between us." Tommy began.

"We've never been to Cincinnati and never seen anything like this. We wanted to know what was inside. So, begging your pardon, ma'am, we'll be on our way," I explained, backing away from Mrs. Trollope and nudging Tommy to move along too.

Mrs. Trollope's face softened as she listened. "Well, today is a slow day. Now mind, I don't believe in giving anything away free of charge. If you'll sweep the walk in front of the museum, I'll let you in for a nickel each."

She started inside the Museum, saying, "If my offer is acceptable, Miss Littsie and Mr. Tommy, follow me."

When we finished our sweeping and gave Mrs. Trollope our nickels, she pointed to a narrow passage lighted by only two small lanterns. Printed on a sign in thick black letters above the entrance was "The Invisible Girl." Inside, a shaky voice demanded, "Who is in my chamber?"

"Littsie O'Donnell," "Tommy O'Brien," we answered together.

"This is an Egyptian burial chamber," said the shaky voice.

"Why are you invisible?" I asked.

"I'm invisible because I choose to be invisible!" the voice replied in a hollow tone that echoed around the room. "Do you wish to go through this Museum? You may find it frightening."

"Yes, we want to go on," Tommy boldly replied.

"Then leave this chamber through the door to your left," the voice instructed.

Carefully we tiptoed into a dim, narrow passage. As we entered the room, we heard strange sounds coming from overhead, then underfoot, then from the walls. Around the room were statues of ugly, twisted figures of men and women and animals, their faces and parts of their bodies revealed by the light from a single lamp.

I looked around and saw the eyes moving in the faces painted on the wall. I screamed in terror and both of us ran down a dark hallway into the next room, "The

Infernal Regions." A man dressed in a red devil's suit greeted us. He leaned down and asked, "Do you like the smell of sulfur?" Laughing a grisly laugh, he pointed to a sign that read, "Whoever enters here, leaves all hope behind." It was a display of what hell may look like.

This room was more horrible than all the others. Skeletons were everywhere. Their bony hands reached out, begging for help. A figure at least seven feet tall sat in a wooden chair under a sign that read, "Minos, Judge of Hell." Behind Minos was a painting of a frozen lake. Rising, floating in the lake, were doomed people, their faces twisted in anguish. There was a devil seated on a rock, dangling the head of an awful, hairy, bulging-eyed monster with large scales hanging from his cheeks.

We heard voices crying out for peace, begging for forgiveness for the evil lives they had lived. Then all the lanterns went out. The sounds came in horrid shrieks, unearthly groans, and terrible cries. A door suddenly swung open. We ran out onto the sidewalk in front of the Museum, as it slammed tight behind us.

Mrs. Trollope, seated at the ticket window, smiled and asked, "Did you enjoy your little visit? Come back sometime, soon," she laughed.

We ran down the street, finally stopping to catch our breath. We agreed that was the best time we had ever had in our whole lives. By my Papa's watch it was nearly 4:00 o'clock, so we headed toward the landing.

On our way, we turned down Walnut Street. In front of a large brick building we saw a group of young girls jumping rope. Others sat on benches reading their books.

"What is that?" I asked Tommy.

"It looks like a school."

A black sign with gold letters above the door read, The Cincinnati Female Academy.

"I went to school in Pittsburgh for half a year," I sighed. "I'd do almost anything to go again."

As we came to the top of the hill on Main Street, we saw Papa smiling and waving to us.

5
A SUDDEN CHANGE OF FORTUNE

*I*N early October, Mama and I stored the vegetables from our garden. We made preserves out of the red tomatoes and pickled the green ones. We tied the onion tops together with string and made wreaths of dried red peppers and hung them on the cabin walls. From the cross beam, we hung sacks filled with seeds for spring planting.

As we worked, I told Mama some of my secret dreams. My special dream was to become a doctor. I told her about the Cincinnati Female Academy and what a fine place it seemed. Mama listened quietly and told me she had seen the school when she visited Cincinnati. She must have told Papa because that week he went to Cincinnati and met with Dr. John Locke, the principal of the Academy. When he got back that day, Papa said he told Dr. Locke, "I have a daughter named Littsie, I mean Elizabeth O'Donnell. She wants to go to school. We are farm folk, new to Columbia, we came from Pittsburgh last spring. When I first came to Cincinnati I passed the Academy and saw the fine young ladies studying their books out front. They are my Littsie's age. She knows her letters and she adds her numbers well. She's a fine, smart girl, Dr. Locke."

Dr. Locke said, "You're going to tell me, you have no money to pay for her tuition."

My father answered, "Yes, that's right. She is a strong young girl and a great help to her mother and me on our farm. Perhaps she could board at the school and work here to pay her tuition."

Dr. Locke agreed it was possible. He needed kitchen help and said he could meet me the next week. But all of that had to wait.

"Why, Grandma Littsie?" Annie, one of my grandchildren, asked.

"It is a long story and hard for me to tell. And it is time for you children to run along to bed."

"Oh, no," the children shouted. "Please, Grandma, just a little bit more," they pleaded.

"Well, maybe just a bit more. But which one of you

will get me a cup of tea?" Annie volunteered, so I settled into my rocking chair and went on with my tale.

You see, when my father left for Cincinnati that morning, the sky was clear and blue. Yet as he got to the city, the sky became gray and overcast and it looked like it would soon start raining.

Late that afternoon, as he headed for home, it started pouring. Papa decided to have supper and wait for it to stop before rowing up river to Columbia.

Everything had been so strange. He asked the cook why there were so few people on the streets, on a market day. The cook replied, "Some say there's a touch of the cholera about. Folks are staying home. Nothing to worry about," the cook laughed. "One person has a little upset stomach and the whole town thinks there's an epidemic."

"Cholera is awful dangerous. It's a killer. It spreads so fast. People get it one day and are dead the next," Papa told him.

As Papa left the hotel, he asked the waiter to fill his water jug for the journey home.

That night when he stumbled into our cabin, Mama ran to him and cried, "Oh Michael, darlin', look at you. You're soaked to the skin. Get out of those wet clothes and into dry ones. You look so pale. Are you all right, darlin'?" Mama asked.

"I don't know, I feel so dizzy and I have an awful cramp in my stomach. Perhaps a cup of your sassafras tea will fix me up, dear Sheila. No need to run to the well for water, there is still some left in my jug."

"The weather was so terrible," Papa said. "The waves on the river this night reminded me of the rough waters in Dingle Bay at home in Ireland. Twice my boat nearly capsized. I thought the old Ohio would swallow me for sure. It's times like this I think of the poem my father taught me as a child. Remember, I taught it to you, Littsie. Come on, now, my girl, how does it go?"

Papa leaned back in his chair as I recited the poem for him:

> *I am the air that kisses the waves,*
> *I am the wave of the deep,*
> *I am the whisper of the surf,*
> *I am the eagle on the cliff,*
> *I am a ray from the pure sun,*
> *I am the grace of growing things,*
> *I am a lake in the rolling meadows,*
> *Who if not I?*

"That poem always gives me peace," Papa whispered.

Before I went to sleep, even though he felt terrible, Papa told me about his meeting with Dr. Locke. All through the night I listened to the sound of his groaning and gagging for air. He was never so sick. I was so worried I hardly slept.

As a thin line of light appeared on the horizon the next morning, my mother gently shook my shoulder. She told me to get dressed and come sit by the fire.

Exhausted and with great sadness she put her arms around my shoulders saying, "Littsie, Papa is very sick.

He complains of terrible pains in his stomach and his arms and legs are like ice. He begs for water and for tea, but no amount of liquid quenches his thirst. What little he can swallow, he vomits out again."

"Maybe some sassafras tea will help him, Mama," I said.

I pulled open the cabin door and ran out into the woods where Megan, Tommy, Sally, Alana and I played so happily that summer. I found the patch of sassafras and tore the rain soaked leaves from their branches. Alana ran after me, wanting to play.

"Not now, Alana, there is no time!" I shouted, as I filled my apron and ran back to the cabin clutching the precious leaves to my chest. Alana was close at my heels.

Megan stood by the fire in her nightgown holding her rag doll by one arm. Alana walked to the far corner of the cabin and lay down, knowing something was wrong. The water in the kettle was boiling as I sprinkled some leaves into the pot. Afraid to ask the question, I whispered, "Will the tea make Papa better?"

Mama put her head into her hands and began to

sob. Megan crept over and put her arms around Mama's knees to comfort her.

"Littsie, your father has cholera. There is no doctor in Columbia, only in Cincinnati."

"Then I'll get a doctor," I told her.

"I must stay with your father. Are you strong enough to take the boat alone on the river?"

"Papa taught me all I need to know. Remember how I steered the flatboat?" I smiled.

"But your father was there to help you. What if, oh, dear God," she sighed, beginning to cry again.

"Mama, it will be all right. I'll find a doctor. I'll bring him back."

Finally, Mama agreed. She put some apples, corn bread and a jug of fresh water in a cloth bag.

"Now, Littsie," she said, cupping my face in her hands, "you're a fine daughter, no parents could be blessed with better. Be sure when you get to Cincinnati, if there are crowds, you stay clear of them. Keep your face covered with your muffler. God give you a safe journey."

She kissed me on both cheeks and hugged me, then she opened the cabin door. "Good-bye, Mama. Good-bye, Megan," I said, hugging them. Then I ran down the path. As I headed down the hill I turned and saw Mama and Megan in the cabin doorway waving.

"Don't worry, Mama! I'll be back with a doctor before noontime," I called, heading down one of Anne Bell Baily's shortcuts to where Papa tied our boat.

Alone on my way to Cincinnati, I thought of my dear sick Papa. Would I find a doctor? I stared at the quiet hills. The sky looked half yellow and half pink, a sign the weather would change and the air would turn much colder. As I steered the boat out into the Ohio River, the strong, swift current carried it toward Cincinnati.

6
THE SEARCH FOR AID

EVERYTHING was so quiet as I rowed past the public landing. There were as many boats tied there as two weeks before, but no one was on them. A hungry looking dog ran along the riverbank at the water's edge. He caught sight of me and stood snarling at my boat. Angrily tossing his head, he sniffed the air then turned and ran off up the landing.

I tied the boat and pushed the food and water Mama gave me into the bow of the boat. Pulling my muffler up around my face, I ran up Main Street. Two pigs in the middle of the empty street, their mouths dripping with mud, dug through a pile of garbage.

Further up Main Street, people hurried passed me wearing mufflers tied tightly around their faces. I called to one man begging him to stop, but he ran away from me. I tried to stop two women walking briskly arm in

THE SEARCH FOR AID

arm, but again they shoved me away.

I staggered through the streets, frightened and exhausted. Pausing to catch my breath in front of a boarding house, I thought surely someone there would help. As I reached for the brass door knocker a man's voice inside shouted, "Stay away! Begone with you! We want no cholera in this house!"

"But, sir, I need help. I need to find a doctor for my father in Columbia. For heaven's sake, help me!" I pleaded.

"Go away, or I'll get my gun!" the voice shouted.

Running out into the street, I saw a man driving a wagon piled high with furniture. I raced toward the wagon, begging the man to stop. He shouted at me to stay away. Running alongside the wagon, as the man was about to take out his whip, the woman sitting next to him begged him to stop for only a moment.

"Sir, it's my Papa. He is sick in Columbia where there are no doctors."

"Child, your efforts are wasted. There are no doctors to help you in Cincinnati. The two or three who remain are so busy they couldn't spare the time to come to Columbia for only one man."

"There are hundreds sick and dying from the dreaded cholera," the woman added.

"It's a epidemic," a young child said, poking his head from under a quilt.

"Get your head back, Matthew!" the man shouted. "Cover the child's face, woman!"

"God save us," the woman sighed.

The man pulled on the reins, causing the horses to rear, "We must get off to the hills, away from this awful place!"

I called out, "But there must be a doctor!"

"Try the Cholera Hospital," the man shouted. And his wife called out over the rattling wagon, "Dr. Drake! Look for a gray horse and a gray buggy in front of the hospital!"

I ran through the deserted streets, past the shops that had so recently lured me with their treasures, past the market, filled with rotting vegetables and meat. On Sixth Street I spotted what looked like a gray horse and buggy.

I went toward it and then up the steps and through the open front door of the building. Seeing no one, I searched the long hall for Dr. Drake. The hospital smelled awful. I looked into a large room where there were rows of cots. Men, women, even children lay covered with sheets or ragged woolen blankets. Some were asleep and others stared with a faraway gaze. The smell, the sounds, the people made me run in terror out of the building and into the street.

A tall man came after me calling, "Stop! Maybe I can help you! I am Dr. Drake."

I turned and cried, "Oh, Dr. Drake, my father is sick in Columbia, with no doctor to care for him."

"I cannot go to Columbia, little one. As you see, so many need me here.

How long has your father been sick?"

"For only a day, but when I left home early this
morning, he was in so much pain."

"Come into the hospital. I will give you some
medicine that may help."

Taking a small blue bottle from a shelf, he said,
"Give him this. It should relax him and stop his pain.
Make sure your father stays in bed. Give him some
sassafras tea and a teaspoon of this medicine. And don't
give him anything to eat until he is better."

"Thank you, doctor, I can't pay you but . . ."

"You better get on your way," he said. "I wish you
Godspeed for your journey."

Carefully, I put the bottle of medicine into my
dress pocket and pulled my muffler up over my face.

Running down Sixth Street, I stopped and looked back at Dr. Drake, as he slowly climbed the hospital steps to go on with the terrible task of caring for those inside.

7
THE STRICKEN CABIN

I rowed close to the shore away from the swift current but I had to stop often to rest. Half way up river, too tired and hungry to go on, I went ashore.

After eating all the food and drinking the water Mama gave me, I lay back on some soft branches and fell asleep. As the sun was setting, I awakened in a panic and rowed to Columbia as fast as I could.

It was pitch dark when I tied the boat at our dock and ran through the woods. When I came to the clearing in front of our cabin, not a single lantern glowed in the windows. This was strange. Mama would be worried when I did not come home. She would have lit a candle to guide my way up the path.

I pushed open the cabin door. A low fire smoldered in the fireplace, giving the room an eerie glow. The same terrible smell of the Cholera Hospital was here. So were the groans, those awful groans.

"Mama, Papa," I called softly. "Mama! Mama!" She was lying on the floor beside my father's bed. I went to her side. Her arms and legs were cold and she held her stomach as if she were in awful pain. At first she did not seem to know me and only stared at something far away.

I poured a little water into a mug. Taking the blue bottle from my pocket, I shook some white powder into it. "Here, Mama, take this medicine. It is from Dr. Drake in Cincinnati."

I rubbed the edge of the mug on her parched lips. Slowly she opened them and swallowed a few drops of the liquid.

I helped my mother into a chair next to the fireplace and built a fresh fire. When I went to my parents' bed to get another blanket for her, I saw my father's face. Oh, my poor, Papa.

"Papa," I tearfully whispered, walking to his side. "Oh, my dear Papa," I wept. Thinking of Mama, I whispered to myself, "Perhaps Mama doesn't know he is dead. I must keep it from her. She must get better, Mama must get better. I've got to make her well."

Carefully I kissed him on both cheeks. I went to Mama and wrapped the blanket around her. With the sassafras leaves I picked that morning, I made some tea. Holding my mother's head, I helped her drink it.

Her fever made her delirious. She tried to speak to me, but she was so weak and her words so confused I couldn't understand her.

"Please, Mama, try not to talk. Hush, hush," I whispered to her. "When you are stronger, you will tell me. Try to rest now, Mama, please, try to rest."

Long into the night I rocked her in my arms. I held her tight, trying to save her, to keep her from my father's awful fate but soon Mama grew quiet.

8
THE LOST CHILD

I made two crosses out of branches from their
favorite tree and placed them at the head of each grave.
Then I slowly walked back into the cabin and looked at
our Bible on the shelf above the fireplace. Opening the
cover, through my tears, I read the Kerry poem:

> *I am the air that kisses the waves,*
> *I am the wave of the deep,*
> *I am the whisper of the surf,*
> *I am the eagle on the cliff,*
> *I am a ray from the pure sun,*
> *I am the grace of growing things,*
> *I am a lake in the rolling meadows,*
> *Who if not I?*

I cried aloud as I remembered Mama and the
dreadful moment when I woke up holding her lifeless
body in my arms. I kept repeating the Kerry poem over
and over. Finally, the words calmed me.

Annie, one of my grandchildren, stopped me from
telling my tale and asked, "Cholera is not around here
anymore is it, Grandma?"

"No, Annie, lucky for us. In 1855 we found out that

cholera comes from polluted water. Oh, my, if only we knew that in 1832."

"Go on with your story, please, Grandma, What happened next?" little Johnnie, my youngest grandchild, insisted.

Well, I'll tell you, I was numb, in a daze, as I held the red plaid blanket I had wrapped around my mother. I carefully folded it and put it on my father's chair. Dr. Drake's medicine I angrily threw into the ashes in the fireplace.

I climbed the ladder to the loft where Megan and I slept. As I walked toward my bed, I tripped over half of the French marker. "Megan!" I shouted. "Where is she?"

I jumped down the ladder and threw the blankets off my parent's bed, thinking she might be there. "Mama was trying to tell me where Megan was. If only I had listened to her," I cried to the empty room. And where was Alana? Had Megan wandered off into the woods? Mama and Papa would have been too weak to call her back. I remembered stories Anne Bell Bailey told of people who got lost in the woods and were never heard from again. What chance would little Megan have?

"Anne Bell Bailey!" I shouted. Surely she'll know where Megan is or at least she'll be able to help me.

I quickly packed the cloth bag with some corn bread and apples in case Megan was hungry when I found her. Without thinking, I picked up half of the French marker and put it into the bag as well.

I left the cabin, closing the door tightly behind me. I went to my parents' graves, bowed my head in silent prayer, begging God to care for them now and to help me find Megan.

As I ran through the woods, I stopped and called, "Megan!" The hills faintly echoed her name.

There was no white flag flying when I got to Anne Bell Bailey's hideaway. All the same, I ran up the hill. Breathlessly, I entered the cave. Once I lit a lantern, as near as I could tell, Anne Bell was gone only a short time because the stones around the fireplace were still warm. The cover looked hastily thrown over the bed, as if she left in a hurry.

Sadly, I walked out of the cave. Perhaps Mama told Megan to go to Tommy's or Sally's and sent Alana along to protect her.

I went to the O'Brien's first. The house was deserted. I tried to push open the cabin door but it would not budge. It was nailed shut.

"They must have gotten scared of the cholera and left," I said to myself. Perhaps Megan is at Sally's. Surely the Tottens would be there. I hurried out onto the main road that led to Columbia.

As I ran up the path toward the house, Sally's father opened the front door and rushed down the steps from the porch. At first I thought he shouted a welcome and had news of Megan. Then I saw the anger in his face as he said, "Stay away! We don't want cholera in this house, Littsie O'Donnell! Stand your ground," he warned. "I've got my wife and children to think of. Where's your ma and pa?"

"They're both dead!" I cried.

"Then don't come a step closer. We can't have cholera in this house!"

"But, Mr. Totten, my sister has gone from our cabin and I thought she might be here," I pleaded.

"Haven't seen your sister, I wish I could help, Littsie, but I can't. Be off with you."

I took a few steps toward him and again he yelled, "Get off this property, Littsie O'Donnell!"

Sally opened the door saying, "Oh, Father, please, won't you help her?" Sally's father pushed her back, "Get inside, you foolish child! Do you want the cholera?" he said, slamming the door behind them.

I turned slowly and stumbled toward the road, dazed and confused, saying aloud, "Who will help me find little Megan?"

I doubled back to the cabin to see if Megan had returned. There was no light in the window. The door was still shut tight. No one was there. It was late afternoon, with little daylight left, still I decided to search the woods near the cabin. When I found no trace of Megan there, I ran frantically into Anne Bell Bailey's forbidden woods. "Never go there," she said. "No one will ever find you."

It was so wild and overgrown, I could not see where I was going. I stumbled, fell and tumbled down to the bottom of a steep hill. Gasping for air, dizzy and

exhausted, I whispered Megan's name and fell into a
deep sleep.

9
ALONE IN THE FOREST

THE next morning, I awakened cold and hungry.
Happily I remembered the food I packed for Megan. Yet
when I opened the bag, I found only the precious
French marker. Its rough edges wore a hole in the bag
and the food had fallen out. Tying a knot in the bottom
of it, so the marker would be safe inside, I began walking
through the woods. "I must find something to eat," I
said to myself, "Anne Bell says there's plenty of food in
the woods, just look for it!"

Pushing through the tall dry weeds, I came to a
shallow stream. I fell to my knees, washed my face and
splashed the clear water into my mouth.

"Anne Bell said we could eat the crawfish who live
under the rocks in the creek." Carefully, I lifted the
rocks and ate the few crawfish I found.

Anne Bell said, "Follow the creek and you'll find
the river." Searching for food, I wandered off into the
hills. If I saw something I might eat on a bush or a tree, I
ran to it foolishly forgetting to keep the creek in sight.

By late afternoon, tired and hungry, I wandered
through the woods. As evening fell, I came to a clearing

where there was a small patch of grass. I ate it, stuffing fistfuls into my mouth. That night I slept on the ground under some fir trees.

I had awful dreams. First there were those in Cincinnati dying of cholera, then Mama and Papa, and then of little Megan frightened and alone in the forest.

The next morning I was so sick to my stomach I imagined I had cholera. "Oh, dear God, not that," I pleaded, "I must get up and start walking."

I pushed further into the thick forest, climbing up one hill and stumbling down another. If I could only get to the top of a very high hill I might have a chance of seeing Megan.

Always looking for food, I turned over every rock and searched every tree for anything I could force into my mouth to keep me alive.

"I will not have the cholera. I will not be sick," I mumbled, "I must keep up my strength."

I wandered for days, becoming like a wild creature, eating whatever I could, even sucking the blood that oozed from my raw fingertips. My clothes were rags, my hair matted and tangled. My mind kept tricking me, as I laughed and shouted until I lost my voice. Finally, early one morning, I heard the sound of water. I staggered toward it.

"Please let it be a creek," I shouted. "Follow the creek, it will lead to the river, Anne Bell Bailey said it would. Megan will be at the river."

I came to a clearing and there it was, a wide creek. I ran into it, splashing, stamping, laughing, shouting for joy, and kicking water every which way. At one point, I slipped and fell. That brought me back to my senses, but only for a moment. Then I put my face down and drank huge gulps of water.

I forced myself to stand and follow the creek. I played games, first counting my footsteps, then putting one foot in front of the other. I marched and sang aloud. Anything to keep moving toward what I hoped would be the river. By dusk I was so confused. The creek seemed to go in circles and since it was getting dark, I decided to sleep on a ledge above the water. I would search again tomorrow.

As I lay on the cold bare stone, clutching the bag that held the precious French marker, I thought, "This is my only memory of Mama and Papa and Megan." I knew I was too weak to go on much longer. My only hope was to find the river.

THE RESCUE

CAPTAIN Malone stood in the pilothouse of the steamboat, peering out into the thick morning fog, complaining to his apprentice, Willy. "Dag blame it! We could have been past Cincinnati by this time, if it weren't for this dag blamed fog! Willy, we need wood for the boilers. Go below and get the wooders. Tell them I'll pull the *Virginia* close to shore so they can get off."

"Yes, sir, Captain," Willy stammered, backing out of the pilothouse. He ran down the stairs to the main deck and called, "Wood pile, wood pile, where are the wooders?" Wooders were passengers who got a cheaper ticket if they agreed to gather wood during their journey. "Wooders! We need wood for the engines."

"Are they off to get the wood, lad?" Malone boomed at Willy.

"Yes, sir, Captain, they put the plank on the shore and are on their way," Willy replied.

"Stay close together," Captain Malone shouted at the wooders, as they stepped onto the riverbank.

"In this pea soup, you can be sure we will," a wooder shouted.

"Let's stick together. We don't want anyone to be left behind," said a rough voice, as another thick cloud of fog swept around them.

Carrying their lanterns high in the air, they looked like a flock of lightening bugs bobbing through the dense fog. "We need a lot of wood to keep those big boilers well fed, now, don't we?" a woman's voice laughed.

"Yes ma'am, we want them to get us to New Orleans as fast as they can!" the rough voice added.

"The logs in this pile are too small," called another wooder.

A German sounding voice called out, "Look, Jameson, what luck! Here are some large logs. Here at the creek is the size we need."

"There are logs here, near this ledge. I bet when the rains come, many big logs wash into this creek."

Holding her lantern close to the ledge, a young French woman, found what seemed like a pile of rags. But when she looked closely, "Ah, Mon Dieu!" she cried, "It is a child!"

Calling to the others for help she dragged my limp

body from the ledge. "See if anyone else is with her," she told them.

They searched and said, "I see no one, just this little girl. She is clutching a filthy bag."

"The child, she is very sick. Yet she holds that soiled bag as if it held a king's ransom."

"Look at her, are you sure she is not dead? We'll take her aboard the boat," said the rough voice.

"We found a little girl!" they shouted to Captain Malone, who stood at the door of the pilot's cabin.

"Leave her there! She may be a local girl, sick with this deadly cholera," he shouted.

"But, Captain, have you no pity!"

"I want nothing to do with pity! I want this boiler filled with wood. I don't see you carrying the logs. Put the girl down gently and do as you were told."

"But, Captain," someone called out again.

Suddenly a woman's voice on the cabin deck, boomed, "Now, what's the commotion? You'll have all the passengers awake!"

"We found a little girl where we were looking for wood. We want permission to bring her on board."

"We'll take care of her, Mrs. Malone."

"All I'm saying is we can't bring children sick with cholera on this boat," insisted the Captain.

Matilda Malone, the captain's wife, was a big, blustery woman and the only one who could tangle with the captain. They got along, most of the time, but the two of them did have some fine arguments. Once Tilly, as Captain Malone called her, got an idea stuck in her head there was no way of prying it out.

"Have you even bothered to look at this poor little dear, Shamus Malone?" Mrs. Malone demanded.

"Well, no," he said, somewhat sheepishly.

"I'll check the girl. If she ain't got the cholera, she's comin' on board," Matilda Malone insisted.

Mrs. Malone examined me for any broken bones, then pushing my matted hair from my face, she checked for a fever.

"She's cold as ice. She's near half dead from lack of food and gettin' lost in them woods, I bet. She's gone woods crazy, that's what I think. As a girl growin' up myself in the Ohio country, I've seen many a one like this and many who did not fare as well," she sighed. "There's not a sign of the disease or of a fever, Captain Malone."

"Well," the Captain said, knowing his wife would have her way, "we don't have much room aboard and she will be another unpaying mouth to feed."

"Oh, poppycock and balderdash, Shamus Malone!" Matilda Malone laughed, "We can put her into that gambler's cabin next to ours. He was to get on in Marietta, but never showed."

"All right, bring her on board. But we're putting her off as soon as she's well," he said.

"All right, Captain," Mrs. Malone replied.

"And the rest of you, don't stand there idle. We can't run a boat without wood. Get moving. The fog is beginning to lift and we can be on our way," Captain Malone shouted, as the wooders gathered more logs.

Matilda Malone carried me in her large, strong arms on to the boat. "What are you doing, you lazy bag of bones?" she demanded of one of the crew.

"Get the steward to bring a bowl of soup and plenty of hot water and towels to the cabin next to the captain's. Tell Annette Fontaine to help me with the lass," Mrs. Malone called over her shoulder, as she climbed the stairs to the cabin deck.

"This matted hair cannot be combed. We'll have to cut it," Mrs. Malone said to herself.

Annette walked into the cabin carrying a pile of white bath towels and a cup of hot soup.

"Take that filthy bag from her, Annette."

As Mrs. Malone offered me some soup, I must have relaxed my grasp and Annette took the bag.

"There now," Annette said, "let us see what she treasures. Why, it's only a broken lead marker, with some French words on it."

"Once the little one has rested, I'm sure she will tell us what it means," Mrs. Malone advised, adding, "put it on the dresser, Annette, in front of her. If she wakes suddenly, she will see it. It seems to mean so much to her."

Taking off her shawl and rolling up her sleeves, Mrs. Malone went to work. She began by cutting my matted hair. Then she bathed my bruised arms and legs. She dressed me in one of Captain Malone's shirts and gently tucked me into bed.

"She seems a different little girl with her hair cut and all the mud washed off, does she not, Mrs. Malone?" Annette smiled.

"She does, Annette. Let's leave her be," Mrs. Malone said, as she turned to leave the room.

"Ah, Mrs. Malone, what about this little trunk with Mr. Wilkins' name on it?"

"It's a strong box, Annette. When we stopped in Marietta, Ohio, a man left it in this cabin for Wilkins. Put it in the closet, back on the top shelf, out of harm's way. We'll leave Wilkins' name on the cabin door. If he gets on board, we'll give the box to him."

I didn't awaken until late the following afternoon. My eyes focused on the window above my bed, where I could just barely make out the sky. Pressing my hands to my temples, fearful I had gone crazy, I sat upright and shouted, "Where am I?"

The door swung open and Mrs. Malone, who had been sitting in a chair outside the cabin door, strode into the room.

"There, there, my child," she comforted, loosening the covers from the bed, "you're all right, you're safe," she said gently. Slowly Mrs. Malone backed out of the room and called, "Annette, the little girl is awake and ready for some food!"

Annette came into the cabin carrying a tray with two slices of bread and a large bowl of chicken broth. I grabbed and ate the bread like a wild animal. I stuffed it into my mouth, gagging on the first few bites. Mrs. Malone tried to spoon the warm broth into my mouth, but I pulled the bowl away and drank from it.

"She has already eaten two slices of bread, should the little one have more?" Annette asked.

"No, too much food is not good for a person who is half starved."

When I finished the soup, I began scrambling around the cabin floor on my hands and knees as if I were looking for something.

"Oh, poor child, she thinks she is in the woods and I reckon she's looking for a place to sleep for the night. Only time and gentle care will help her now," Mrs. Malone sighed.

THE RETURN TO HEALTH

As Mrs. Malone carried a basket of fruit to my cabin, the Captain said, "If I'd taken on ten more passengers, no one could eat as much as this child! I hope she'll be herself soon and she'll stop wearing my good white shirts for night gowns," he concluded, heading off to the pilot's cabin.

For six days Mrs. Malone used her ways to cure me

of the "woods crazies". Early one morning, memories of being on the flatboat came back to me. I even imagined I was on a steamboat on the river.

"My mind is playing tricks on me," I whispered. "If only I can rest. When I awaken, I'll find the river and Megan will be there."

I closed my eyes again. Slowly I knew the sound I heard was truly the sound of a paddle wheel churning water. I was not lost in the woods but in a beautiful white room. Across the room was a window. Under the window was a wooden chair in front of a writing table and next to it was a little red velvet couch.

I struggled to get out of bed but the covers were tucked under the mattress. I was so weak, I fell back on my pillow. Looking straight ahead I saw the French marker propped up on the dresser.

"Mama, Papa," I cried, "and Megan, oh, Megan, I couldn't find you in those frightful woods."

Mrs. Malone rushed into my room and threw her arms around me saying, "Well, my little one, you are awake this fine morning. You look better than you did when we found you under the creek ledge. I bet you'd like to get out of this bed, wouldn't you, my fine young one?" she laughed, pulling on the sheets.

"Now let me look at you. Here, wrap this shawl around your shoulders and put these socks on your feet. Sit at the desk by the window. You can look out at the river while you have your breakfast."

"Yes, ma'am. I'm afraid I don't know where I am. I

feel I must be dreaming."

Annette came in smiling, "Oh, it is good to see you awake, my little one. How do you feel today?"

"Much better, I guess, ma'am," I shyly replied.

The sunshine streamed into the room through the open window above the desk. I could look down at the river and the distant shore. "I am on a boat!" I exclaimed. "But where am I going?"

"One question at a time," said Mrs. Malone.

"What is your name child?"

"I'm Littsie O'Donnell and I live in Columbia, Ohio. My folks died of cholera. I couldn't find my little sister, Megan, even though I searched everywhere for her," I said bursting into tears.

"There, there, take your time," Annette said, stroking my head.

"Hold on, Littsie O'Donnell. I told you one question and one answer at a time. Use your napkin to blow your nose. Now the question is, are you hungry? There's time enough to tell us your troubles. I find they're easier to face on a full stomach."

"You can start eating as I tell you about myself. I'm Mrs. Matilda Malone and the boat you're on, is the finest steamboat on the Ohio, the Mississippi, or any river for that matter. My husband, Captain Shamus Malone, is the Captain. You'll meet him later."

"But how did I get here?"

"I'll let Annette tell you the whole story. Now I have chores to do. You finish your meal, Littsie

O'Donnell, and take a nap afterwards. This afternoon we'll take a walk around the deck."

Matilda Malone walked to the cabin door. As she opened it she turned and said, "Mrs. Matilda and Captain Shamus Malone are pleased to have you as our guest on the steamer, *Virginia*!"

"My little one, I will tell you where my husband, Robert, and I found you three days ago. Oh, and my name is Annette Fontaine."

As Annette was about to begin her story, I put my hand to my head and felt my short hair.

"It was so matted and tangled, we had to cut it," Annette explained.

The warm sun, the food, even sitting in the chair and talking made me so tired. Annette took the shawl from my shoulders and helped me into bed. As she left my cabin, she met Mrs. Malone.

"Look what I've got! I was talking with the passengers on the hurricane deck about Littsie. Some of them said they had extra clothes and could spare a dress or two and some shoes for her. They were so generous. I have five lovely dresses and there are socks and even some underwear. Not the kind of clothes an Ohio farm girl is used to," Mrs. Malone laughed, "But I'm sure they'll do."

"Ah, Mrs. Malone, they are so beautiful! She will love them. There is Robert. I will tell him the good news about the little one."

"I am glad to hear she is all right," Robert said to

Annette, as they walked together on the main deck. "Does she know we are headed for New Orleans?"

"No one has told her," replied Annette. "I don't know what she will do when we arrive there. The Malones cannot take care of her on the steamboat."

"Perhaps you and Mrs. Malone will find a way to help her?" Robert smiled.

12
AN ANSWER

"**MISS** Littsie, I think you're ready for a stroll on the cabin deck with Annette and me," said Mrs. Malone, putting the pile of dresses on the couch. "You can wear this pink silk or the blue velvet."

I could hardly believe my eyes. I never saw such beautiful clothes.

"I have some petticoats, warm socks and underwear given to you too," Mrs. Malone said, as she sorted through the clothing. "And here are the bonnets that match the dresses," she showed me, pulling them from the bottom of the pile. When I was dressed, Mrs. Malone told me I looked like a fine young lady in my blue velvet dress and bonnet.

"Is Littsie your real name?" asked Mrs. Malone.

"No ma'am, I am named after my great Aunt

Elizabeth Pierce McIntyre," I said. As I thought of my family, I began to cry. "Oh, Mama, Papa and dear little Megan, if only you were here!"

"Tell us what happened," Mrs. Malone said, sitting down on the bed next to me.

I told her about going to Cincinnati to find a doctor and how my parents died of cholera and that my sister Megan and Alana were both lost in the woods or dead.

"And the marker?" Annette asked.

"I found it on the banks of the Ohio River just before we got to Columbia. I took it from the cabin without even thinking. Now it is my only reminder of my family. As soon as I'm well, I'm going to search for my sister. When the boat gets to Cincinnati, you will tell me, won't you?" I asked.

Mrs. Malone looked at Annette and then at me saying, "Littsie, we're past Cincinnati. We're a few miles from Memphis and heading for New Orleans."

"But I have to go to Cincinnati!" I shouted.

"There's no way you can do that. You did everything you could in Columbia, visiting the people you knew and asking for your sister. Then you wandered around the woods looking everywhere and you were lost and could have died. Am I right, Littsie? Answer me!" she demanded.

"Yes, ma'am, I did," I mumbled sadly.

"I didn't hear that. I want you to say it like you believe it, young lady," Mrs. Malone almost shouted.

"Yes, ma'am, I did look everywhere and I couldn't find my sister," I shouted back.

"All right, that's more like it. I'm a woman who's as practical as night and day, Miss Elizabeth Pierce McIntyre O'Donnell," Mrs. Malone said, as she leaned toward me with her hands on her hips. "When there's a problem, I aim to solve it. You're on a boat heading for New Orleans. You cannot get off to find your sister and you and I know a couple of other facts."

"An animal might have gotten her," I interrupted.

"Right you are! Or maybe she died of cholera."

"Maybe she's wandering in the woods."

"And there is no way you can give her a hand," stated Mrs. Malone. "If she's dead, she's dead and that's a fact. If a friendly neighbor took her in, then you'll meet up with her again somewhere."

I tried to interrupt, but Mrs. Malone had an idea stuck in her head and as I would soon learn, no one could pry it out.

"Megan can't be helped by a child who is sick and needs to take care of herself."

"But, Mrs. Malone, I don't know anyone in New Orleans! Who will take care of me?" I cried.

Mrs. Malone replied, "We're not in New Orleans yet, Littsie. We have three days before we get there. I'm sure something will turn up. Meanwhile, we're wasting a perfectly good afternoon. Dry your eyes and Annette and I will show you the grandeurs of the steamboat, *Virginia*," she said, offering me her arm. She opened the cabin door and we strolled onto the deck.

As the three of us looked out over the river, across the low grassy hills on the far bank, I felt the chill of the November wind on my face. The river smelled like a daylong rain in the woods near my family's cabin. I stood for a moment watching as the boat moved through the water. We passed farms and villages. Children ran along the bank, waving to the steamer.

"There on the deck below is where we stay," said Annette.

"Couldn't you get a cabin?" I asked.

"Ah, mais oui, we could have gotten one, but we wanted to save our money. So we help on the boat for the price of our fare," she smiled, as we walked down the deck.

"Let's go here into the dining room," Mrs. Malone said, leading me through an open doorway.

The dining room was decorated like a palace. The red wool carpets were as soft as the grass in a summer field. Around the room hung glittering crystal chandeliers. Oh, it was something!

We went to the far end of the room to a place called the "ladies cabin" where women sat around small tables, playing cards, and drinking tea.

Mrs. Malone said in her booming voice, "Ladies, I'd like you to meet Miss Littsie O'Donnell. She's heading to New Orleans with us."

The women said hello to me and went on with their gossip, cards, and tea. Mrs. Malone saw an empty chair near the windows.

"Sit here, my fine young friend, and I'll pull this
table close to you for your tea. I'll bring you just one
cake. I don't want you to spoil your appetite for dinner."

The sun was just setting behind the low rising hills.
The sky was a soft orange, a perfect November evening.
Gladys O'Sullivan, who was playing the piano, walked
over saying, "So this is your latest charge, Matilda?
Come now, Littsie, with a name like O'Donnell are you
from Ireland," she smiled.

"Yes, ma'am. Mama, Papa, my sister Megan and
me, we were all born in Dingle in County Kerry. Would
you have known the O'Donnells?"

Smiling she answered, "No, lass. I'm from Kinsale,
County Cork. I've been here in the states for more years
than I care to count. I married a man who was a farmer.
Then he found he liked playing cards on the steamers
up and down the Ohio and Mississippi Rivers. It's not
the life I would have chosen, but to tell the truth, he's
better at cards than he was at farming and I have a
chance to enjoy your grand company," she smiled.

A woman with a southern accent said, "We heard
your parents died, and perhaps your little sister as well,
in the cholera epidemic in Ohio."

"Yes, ma'am, I'm sorry to say that's true."

"The plague that struck Cincinnati was in New
Orleans too. It killed so many in the Crescent City," the
woman continued.

"My sister and I are returning, from Cairo, Illinois.

Our husbands told us it is safe now," a second woman said. "In August there was a violent tornado that swept over New Orleans. The Creoles thought that it was a sign a disaster was about to strike us."

Reaching into her sewing basket she took out a piece of paper, "Here is the letter my husband sent us only two days ago. He is a minister in New Orleans and helped to bury the dead. Mrs. O'Sullivan, would you like to read his letter?"

Mrs. O'Sullivan sat across from me and read the letter to all the women in the cabin.

November 14, 1832

My Dearest Emma,

The newspapers all report there were six thousand deaths in the twelve days the plague raged from October 25 to November 6. Many more died but there is no record of their death.

During those days, as I offered to help those in need, I saw people struggling with the illness. One evening as I walked near the river I met two men. They were forced off a steamer because they had cramps and convulsions, the symptoms of cholera. Their hands and feet were cold and blue and an icy perspiration streamed down their faces. One of them told me he was so thirsty it seemed as if an iron bar lay across his throat.

Others I saw were rigid, blackened corpses, awaiting the

arrival of a hearse to take them to their final resting place.

To make life even more unbearable, in the midst of this nightmare, the mayor ordered barrels of tar and pitch to be burned at every street corner. And he had cannons fired all day and all night when the plague was at its worse. He thought the burning and the cannon blasts would purify the air.

As I walked my nightly rounds to visit sick parishioners, the flames from the burning tar lighted the streets and river. I could see everything as distinctly as in daytime. The constant firing of the cannons, the corpses, the fires, all made the city a hellish place.

At this date, November 14, I am happy to report, the plague has ended and I believe it is safe for you and your sister to return to New Orleans.

"Well, that's quite a tale!" exclaimed Mrs. Malone. "Glad we were not near New Orleans for the likes of that. We were lucky to miss the cholera epidemic in both Cincinnati and New Orleans."

"I think we need a little music. What do you say, lass," Mrs. O'Sullivan said, trying to put everyone into a happier mood. "I'll play your favorite songs while you sip your tea and eat your cake."

"That's kind of you, ma'am," I said. "Do you know 'Mick McGuire', or 'The Rattling Bog'?"

"Of course, child," she said, and began to play my favorite songs.

"We're about to ring the bell for dinner, Littsie. I'm sure if you need anything, Mrs. O'Sullivan will help you. Annette will help me set up for tonight's meal," Mrs. Malone said.

I looked out the window. Far below was a family on a flatboat struggling to keep it steady in the swells of the *Virginia*. I smiled as the man shook his fist at the steamer, just as Papa would have done.

As I thought about my family, I heard my name softly whispered. I turned and saw a tall man with a white beard, wearing a captain's hat.

"I beg your pardon, miss. I'm Captain Shamus Malone. Will you join us for dinner?

"Thank you, sir," I said, smiling up at him.

Seven people sat at the Captain's table. There was Mrs. Gladys O'Sullivan and her husband, John Duggan O'Sullivan, a tall handsome man with a black beard. Mr. and Mrs. Harris Rogers, plantation owners from Charleston, South Carolina, traveling to New Orleans to visit their married daughter. Then there was Mrs. Malone and Dr. Harold Gilbert, a short stocky man with sandy colored hair.

"Littsie, sit next to Dr. Gilbert," Captain Malone said. "Well, Littsie," the Captain continued, "I was afraid you had cholera, but you didn't, thank heavens. My dear wife was right. She did a good job of nursing you. She told me your story. You are a brave child for all you went through." Pointing across the room he said, "Littsie, the *Virginia* has the best food on the Mississippi and some of it is on those tables over there. Have whatever you please."

The tables were piled high with more food than I ever saw in one place. There were meats, and whole steaming fish, chickens glazed with honey, baskets of bread and biscuits, dishes filled with jams and butter. Large bowls overflowed with apples and pears and next to them were cakes and pies.

"Captain," I sighed, "I don't know what I want."

"Then I'll tell the waiters what to bring you for a hearty meal," Mrs. Malone said.

Dr. Gilbert asked, "How are you today, Littsie?"

"I'm much better, thank you."

"Tell us, Dr. Gilbert, why are you traveling on the *Virginia* at this time of year?" asked Mrs. Rogers.

"And where is your beautiful wife, Mary?" added Mrs. O'Sullivan.

"I am sad to say she died in childbirth only six months ago."

"How terrible," said Mrs. Rogers.

"You have our sympathy, Dr. Gilbert," Mrs. Malone said sadly.

"I've been in Memphis the past week settling her estate and trying to comfort her family. She was a dear, kind woman. We all loved her and miss her."

Mrs. Rogers hesitated, "How is the baby?"

"We lost her as well," he replied.

"And your other two children, how are they?" Mrs. O'Sullivan asked.

"They are better than they were just after their
mother's death. Mary's older sister, Gertrude, came to
live with us to care for the children and the house.
During the cholera epidemic Gertrude took the
children to stay with relatives in St. Louis. I don't know
what I would have done without her. I worked night and
day to help the sick and dying."

"How old are your children, Dr. Gilbert?" asked
Mrs. Rogers.

"Kevin is five and Barbara is just seven."

"Dr. Gilbert, perhaps you could use someone close
to their age to watch over them," Mrs. Malone observed.
"I know a girl who could do just that."

"She must be able to take orders and get along with
Gertrude."

"Perhaps Miss Littsie O'Donnell could be your
governess," suggested Mrs. Malone.

Confused I said, "To tell you the truth, I don't
know what a governess is."

"Let me ask you a few questions, Littsie," Dr.
Gilbert said. "Have you ever cared for little children?"

"Yes, Dr. Gilbert. I took care of my sister, Megan," I
began to cry as I thought of her.

"Go on, child," Dr. Gilbert insisted.

" . . . and neighbor children. I kept them out of
trouble. I played games with them and taught them their
letters and numbers."

"Could you follow orders, even when the orders are
hard to follow?"

"Well, sir, Dr. Gilbert, I'd do my best. I was a help to my Mama and Papa. I can cook, spin, and weave. I can preserve vegetables and fruit. I can cut down trees and sow seeds. I know about Indians in the Ohio country from my friend Anne Bell Bailey and . . . "

"Littsie, hold on," Dr. Gilbert laughed. "I think you are fine. Will you live with my family in New Orleans and help with the care of my children?"

"Yes," Dr. Gilbert, but how long would I stay?"

"You may leave whenever you wish. Although you must tell Aunt Gertrude and myself your plans."

"Littsie, you cannot return to Ohio until spring. Because of the ice, there are few boats on the river," Captain Malone explained.

"I want more than anything in this world to find my sister, Dr. Gilbert. Since I can't do that now, thank you for your kind offer. I will be your children's gov. . ."

"Governess," Dr. Gilbert smiled.

" . . . governess for your Kevin and Barbara."

Mrs. Malone smiled happily at Littsie and Dr. Gilbert, pleased with this turn of events.

"And so that is why you know so much about New Orleans, Grandma Littsie," little Anne smiled.

"That's right, Anne. But now, children, it's late and time for bed. Tomorrow I'll tell more of my story."

THE STRANGER

THE wind blew and the snow fell throughout the night. Deep drifts lined the city streets. Snow and ice covered the bridges that crossed the Ohio River, making it impossible for horse drawn wagons to deliver their heavy loads of goods. And, of course, on such a day, the children could not get out and go to school. Since they would be at home, my grandchildren begged me to go on with my story. It was a perfect day for me to finish it. So I asked the older children to get some logs for the fire. When they brought them in, I put them into the fireplace and stirred the hot ashes so the logs would catch fire and the room would be nice and warm. Settling into my favorite chair, I went on with my tale.

Let me see, where was I, ah, yes. It was Willy, Captain Malone's apprentice, who led a passenger into the pilothouse. Then Willy ran down the steps, leaving the door open. That's how I heard the Captain's booming voice say, "Wilkins? Wilkins paid for his passage but he never came on board. Someone put a strong box with his name on it in the cabin when we stopped in Marietta, Ohio. We left his name on the cabin door in case he joined us along the way. For now, Littsie, the child we picked up on the riverbank, is staying in his cabin."

"I'll tell you Captain Malone, Wilkins is a bad one. He'd as soon slash a man's throat with a dinner knife than take supper with him."

"Glad we didn't meet up with the likes of Mr. Wilkins," Captain Malone replied.

"It's been a quiet trip for you, has it, Captain?"

"Yes, and for that I'm grateful," he laughed.

"No races?"

"No, not the *Virginia*, sir, I wouldn't race my boat, never even been in a race. But I've seen my share of them. I've seen steamers explode and sink. The boats were gone in a matter of minutes with many of their crew and passengers drowned. Those are tragedies I'll never forget."

Just then, Mrs. Malone came down the deck with a girl about my age. "Littsie, come here. I'd like you to meet our new chambermaid, Miss Maddie Paterson," Mrs. Malone said.

"Pleased to meet you, Miss Maddie Paterson."

Maddie was a pretty girl with long straight coal black hair. Her haunting gray eyes stared in a cold, almost cruel way.

"Maddie will help you whenever you need anything, Littsie."

"I don't want to trouble her, Mrs. Malone."

"Nonsense, child. The boat docks in New Orleans tomorrow. If you need any help with your packing, just ask Maddie. She will take Annette's place, when the *Virginia* gets to New Orleans."

"Littsie, go with Maddie to the main deck, find Annette so she can show Maddie her duties."

"I'll be glad to, Mrs. Malone," I replied.

Maddie wore a black cotton dress that was too long for her and she kept tripping over the hem. I offered to sew it for her but she snapped, "Well, isn't that sweet! Thank you, I don't need any help from the cabin passengers." I was confused by her answer, so we didn't talk anymore.

That night, as I went to bed, I left my cabin door open. There was a party in the dining room and I wanted to hear the music as the cabin passengers enjoyed their last night on the *Virginia.*

Finally, I fell asleep but was awakened by someone moving around in my cabin. A man's voice whispered words that sounded evil and angry. "I know something is in this cabin for me and I aim to have it," the voice said aloud. He sat on my bed, saying, "Tell me where you stashed it or you'll be saying howdy-do to your maker!"

Light from a lamp on the deck came through the half open cabin door. The man's face was partly hidden by the broad brim of his green felt hat. He put his hand over my mouth to keep me from screaming and held the long blade of his knife to my throat.

His dark piercing eyes flashed with sudden terror as he

heard passengers walking down the deck outside my cabin.

He angrily plunged his knife into my bed. Backing out of the room, he whispered, "Not a word of this to anyone, not a word to a living soul." He closed the cabin door tightly behind him.

I was too frightened to move, too terrified to leave my cabin. I couldn't get help for fear the man was outside in the shadows waiting for me. I hardly slept that night. I lay staring at the window above my desk, watching for dawn's first gray light. Finally, exhausted, I fell asleep.

When I awakened, I believed the terrible man was only a bad dream. I gasped when I saw the deep gash his knife made in my mattress. "Yikes!" I shouted, "he almost got me!" Chills raced through me at I thought of the man's eyes as he turned and left the cabin, his knife pointed at me.

I dressed as fast as I could and ran to the dining room where I found Captain Malone and Mr. O'Sullivan at the Captain's table. Looking cautiously around the room before I entered, I ran to the table and asked if I could sit with them.

"Of course you can, Littsie. Sit in this chair next to me," Captain Malone said.

"You don't seem too happy this morning," Mr. O'Sullivan commented, spreading raspberry jam on a corn muffin. "Here, Littsie, try this. It's sure to put the sparkle back in your eyes."

Captain Malone watched me eat tiny bites of the muffin and asked, "Is there something bothering you, lass?"

"Captain, something horrible happened to me last night. A man came into my cabin and tried to kill me."

The captain burst out laughing, saying, "Oh, Littsie, no tall tales."

"Then come with me."

I led the captain and Mr. O'Sullivan to my cabin. When I showed them the knife mark, the Captain asked, "But why didn't you cry out?"

"I was too afraid."

"We'll find the demon who did this," said Mr. O'Sullivan angrily.

"And we'll see he gets a lashing he won't soon forget," agreed the Captain.

"Sir, since the boat docks in New Orleans in only a few hours, I'd sooner you didn't do that. He threatened to slit my throat if I told 'a living soul'."

The Captain hesitated, "Perhaps you're right. I don't want any harm to come to you. But you must tell me exactly what he looked like. We'll keep an eye out for him."

"He won't stay on the boat after trying something like that," assured Mr. O'Sullivan.

"Don't think about that hateful man," advised Captain Malone. "There's many bad people on the steamers. I'll be sure the stewards keep a more watchful eye," promised Captain Malone.

14
ARRIVAL IN NEW ORLEANS

As I stood on the deck, the *Virginia* docked at Red Church, Louisiana, a town twenty-four miles from New Orleans. I watched the passengers leave the boat. Just as I started back to my cabin, I saw him, the man who threatened me with his knife. He ran down the gangplank carrying a small trunk, just like the one I saw far back in the closet in my room. A chill shot through every bone in my body as he jumped onto the bank. His green felt hat was pulled down to cover his face. He looked back, his dark piercing eyes searched the upper decks of the boat, then he dashed up the landing.

Mr. O'Sullivan ran down the gangplank and caught the man at the top of the landing. "Get the sheriff!" Mr. O'Sullivan shouted. "He's stolen Wilkins' strong box!"

Minutes later, some men rushed toward Mr. O'Sullivan. They handcuffed the man in the green felt hat and led him away. I knew I wouldn't be running into him again and for that I was grateful.

When I heard the stewards call out "New Orleans, New Orleans, about to dock in New Orleans!" I hurried to my cabin to finish packing.

Dr. Gilbert knocked on my door saying, "Littsie, let me help you with your baggage. It's time we headed for the main deck."

Mrs. Malone hugged me as we left the boat. I thanked her for all she had done for me. "Perhaps, in the spring," she smiled, "you can go back to Cincinnati on the *Virginia.*"

"I wouldn't go on any other boat."

"Good-bye, Littsie, it was good having you aboard!" Captain Malone called from the pilot's cabin.

I waved to him saying, "Thank you, Captain, for all your kindness."

The Fontaines followed Dr. Gilbert and me down the gangplank. As they made their way through the crowd on the landing, they called, "Good luck, Littsie. Be well, little one."

"Merci, merci," I called back.

I stayed close to Dr. Gilbert as he made his way through the crowds. When we reached a clearing, Dr. Gilbert tried to stop a carriage. As I stood next to him, I took a deep breath. The air was filled with the smell of fish and Mississippi River mud. As I looked around, I saw bales of cotton, some piled as high as a three-story building. There were bags of fragrant coffee beans and spices, stacks of furniture and farming tools. Beggars and medicine men, Indians, sailors, boatmen, fine ladies dressed in satin gowns and men in finely tailored suits, were all here on the wide flat cobblestone landing. A blind man pushed a cart filled with pretzels he sold to passengers waiting for carriages. Black women sat fanning themselves behind wooden tables filled with pineapples and bananas and candied apples.

Then I saw the worst sight I have ever seen. There was a long line of black men, all chained one to the other, walking slowly in single file down the gangplank of a large ship. Their heads were bent low. Their naked black bodies glistened with sweat as they moved. Some limped, others stumbled under the weight of the heavy chains stretched through metal collars worn around their necks, hands and ankles.

"Come along, Littsie, we will never get a carriage here. I'm sure there will be one in front of the Customs House on Canal Street. It's only a few blocks away," Dr. Gilbert said, heading up the landing.

As I hurried after him, I turned to look again at the black men. What a sad and terrible life they had.

"But, Dr. Gilbert, did you see that?"

"Yes, they are slaves from Africa. They'll be on the slave bloc on Esplanade Street this very afternoon," he said seriously.

Out of breath, I pleaded, "But that's terrible! Doesn't that make you sick and angry to see people treated that way, Dr. Gilbert?"

"What I think isn't important. There are those who believe in slavery."

"Well, I think it's wrong!"

"You may think that, Miss Littsie O'Donnell, but I would keep my thoughts to myself here in New Orleans.

I don't keep slaves and I don't talk about slavery because it's best people mind their own business as to how they run their homes. I don't care to discuss the matter any further, Littsie," he said, and I knew the subject was closed for him. But I never would forget the sight of all those men chained together.

"Come along," Dr. Gilbert urged, as he waved to a maroon carriage pulled by a beautiful rust colored horse.

The day was sunny and warm as we rode in the open carriage through the narrow streets to Dr. Gilbert's house. Dr. Gilbert had the driver stop the carriage at the front door of the white three-story Gilbert house.

It was grand. Each clear glass window went almost from floor to ceiling. They had elegant pink and rose flowered drapes. The parlor was filled with velvet covered chairs and couches.

As we walked into the hall, I heard a child cry out, "Hurrah, Father's home!"

There were leaping, jumping footsteps on the stairs as two blond haired children, a boy and a girl, ran down the stairs and into their father's open arms. When they looked at me, I said, "I am Miss Elizabeth O'Donnell. Pleased to meet you," making an awkward curtsey.

Putting his arms around the children's shoulders, Dr. Gilbert said that I would be their governess.

"Where did you live?" Barbara asked.

"Do you know any ghost stories?" Kevin interrupted.

As I tried to answer, a tall black man walked into

the parlor from the back of the house.

"Welcome home, Dr. Gilbert," he said, heartily shaking the doctor's hand.

"Thank you, Dan, it's good to be home. Littsie, this is Mr. Daniel Joseph Powell. He works for us in our home and is also my aide in my clinic. Daniel is the best medical aide in the whole of New Orleans."

"How do you do, I'm pleased to know you," I said again with a little curtsey.

A thin white woman, with gray hair came down the stairs. "Welcome home, Harold," she said quietly.

"Ah, Gertrude, thank you," Dr. Gilbert smiled.

She stood on the landing looking down at me. With her arms folded tightly across her chest she said, "Who is this little stranger?"

"Miss Elizabeth O'Donnell, I would like you to meet Mrs. Gertrude Fallon, or Aunt Gertrude, as we call her," Dr. Gilbert replied. "Aunt Gertrude, my dear wife's sister, is a great help to all of us."

Walking to Aunt Gertrude and taking her hand, Dr. Gilbert continued, "Gertrude, Littsie's life has been sad. Both of her parents died in the cholera epidemic in Ohio last October. Her four year-old sister, Megan, wandered from the family's cabin and Littsie does not know where she is. Since we have gone through the same nightmare with the cholera epidemic, we know the pain she feels."

"I am sorry to hear about your parents and your sister," Aunt Gertrude said softly. "How long will Littsie stay with us, Harold?"

"In the spring she hopes to go back to Ohio. While she is here she will do whatever she can to help you. She can take care of the children too. She might even be able to help out in the clinic."

"Miss O'Donnell, ah, Littsie, I can use some help with the children and I know Sweet Bell, our cook, can use an extra pair of hands in the kitchen as well."

"And any cleaning or cooking," I interrupted.

"But, I will not have any back talk. Do you understand? You will follow my orders to the letter."

"I'll do my best, ma'am," I replied. At this, I bowed my head. I was ready to burst into tears. I thought of how alone I was and how much I missed my family and our simple home in Columbia.

15
MY LIFE AS A GOVERNESS

Dr. Gilbert, the children, Dan Powell and Sweet Bell were so kind. Even Aunt Gertrude and I got along fine since I did everything just the way she wanted. Before I came to the Gilbert's, Sweet Bell did all the cooking, cleaning, and marketing. She was glad to have a helper. Sweet Bell took me to the French Market on the Public Road at the levee and showed me how to shop. After a few days, I went alone. I was always one of the first customers. Sweet Bell gave me her basket to carry the freshest fruits and vegetables as they were unloaded from the boats or brought by farmers from the towns near New Orleans.

I enjoyed going to market. There were so many different kinds of people in New Orleans, Creole, Spanish, American and, of course, French. There were French food and French music and French holidays. I began to understand that the explorers who put my French marker on the shores of the Ohio probably came from here. For some reason, my marker made me feel as if I belonged in New Orleans, if only for a little while.

I heard languages I never would have heard in Columbia. And sights, oh my! There were cockfights, French theatre, great fancy balls and, once in awhile, I even saw men dueling with swords. And every night at 9:00 o'clock a cannon was fired. It was the signal for soldiers and sailors to get off the streets or risk going to jail. Usually too, it was the sign for the children to go to bed. I loved the color and excitement of New Orleans.

Most of all I liked working in the clinic with Dan Powell. He taught me about herbal medicine. I learned that the foxglove plant is good for circulation, that powdered cinchona bark will help malaria, that red clover tea will aid indigestion and that sometimes the juice of dandelions will make warts go away.

"So that's where you learned all that," interrupted Anne. "I always wondered how you knew so much about medicine, Grandma."

And I learned a little Latin from Dr. Gilbert too. Aunt Gertrude, bless her, taught me what was expected of a southern young lady. She showed me how to smile and be gracious to Dr. Gilbert's patients, how to make small talk and even how to curtsey.

I liked to watch Dr. Gilbert use his skills when he examined patients and when he fixed their broken bones. I often thought that, if things were different, I would like to work for Dr. Gilbert.

Now I wasn't the only one learning. I took Barbara and Kevin for hikes. I showed them what they could find to eat in the woods, how to catch rabbits and skin them, all the things I learned at home and especially what Anne Bell Bailey taught me. The children loved our hikes but Aunt Gertrude wasn't all that happy about my outdoor lessons. She complained to Dr. Gilbert who calmed her by saying he enjoyed the woods too and the first free day he had he would join us for a lesson.

As the days and weeks passed, I often thought of Megan. I knew I must leave New Orleans and go back to Cincinnati to search for her.

One day, when Dr. Gilbert finished his work and was in his study reading, I told him I was worried about Megan and I needed to find her. Since it was almost spring, the steamboats would be running north again.

"I was afraid that was what you were thinking," he said, "but, in my own selfish way, I hoped you wouldn't go. You are such a big help to all of us. You have a real gift for medicine. Perhaps one day you can use your talent as a nurse or even a doctor."

It was as if Dr. Gilbert had read my mind. At that time, that is what I wanted to do more than anything, but first I had to find Megan.

"Could I ask your help, Dr. Gilbert?"

"Why, of course, Littsie, what is it?"

"I need to write a letter to Dr. Locke at the Cincinnati Female Academy. I want to ask him if I can board and go to school there when I return to Cincinnati."

"Here, sit at my desk," he said, as he pulled over a large chair next to his. "We'll write the letter and send it in the morning." This is what we wrote:

February 20, 1833

Dear Dr. Locke,

My name is Miss Elizabeth O'Donnell, although my family always called me Littsie. Last October, you met my father, Michael O'Donnell. He told me you needed kitchen help at the Academy and in return for doing this work I could get room, board and schooling. Both my mother and father died in the cholera epidemic in Columbia last fall. My sister, Megan, wandered off and is either in Columbia or Cincinnati or dead of the cholera herself. Through the kindness of friends, I am safe here in New Orleans working as a governess for a doctor's family. I want to return to Cincinnati in early April. I am truly grateful, if your offer of work and schooling is still good. Please write to me at the home of Dr. Harold Gilbert, Bourgoyne and St. Ann, New Orleans, Louisiana.

Yours sincerely,
Littsie O'Donnell

March is a beautiful month in New Orleans. Flowers such as pink, purple and red azaleas, white magnolias and gardenias are everywhere. One sunny morning I bought a bouquet of spring flowers in the market to bring home to Aunt Gertrude. When I got there, Barbara shouted, "We've been waiting for you, Littsie!"

"Look what came for you!" Kevin said, jumping up and down, pointing to a letter Sweet Bell held in her hand.

It was from Dr. Locke. My hands were shaking as I read:

March 10, 1833

Dear Miss Littsie O'Donnell,

I remember your father, Michael O'Donnell. I am sorry to hear of his death and that of your mother. Please accept my sympathy. The position your father and I discussed in

*October is yours. Please come to the Cincinnati Female
Academy when you arrive in Cincinnati. If you can do
the work, you will board here and take classes. I look
forward to meeting you.*

Best wishes for a safe return to Cincinnati,
Dr. John Locke

We were all so happy. Sweet Bell grabbed my hands
and we danced around the kitchen.

When Dr. Gilbert came home for lunch, I read the
letter to him. When I finished, he told me that since he
and Aunt Gertrude knew I would be returning to
Cincinnati they had a surprise for me. They led me into
the parlor where Dr. Gilbert pulled a large trunk from
the closet.

"Go ahead, Littsie, open it," he smiled.

"Oh, thank you," I said, "but you see Dr. Gilbert, I
can do just fine with my small bag. I don't have enough
things to put into a trunk."

"Yes, you do!" yelled Kevin. "Open it, go on, open it!"

I was a little frightened at the thought of what
might be inside. Knowing Kevin, it could be a snake.
Slowly I opened the trunk, ready to slam it shut if I
needed to. But there was no reason to be afraid. The
trunk was filled with hats and dresses and coats, aprons,
shoes and boots, even an umbrella. Everything a young
city girl would need.

All I could say was, "How beautiful! How kind of

you! Oh, thank you!" as I looked at each piece.

"Aunt Gertrude had a lot of fun doing the shopping," said Dr. Gilbert. "You will be a well dressed young lady. Aunt Gertrude has seen to that."

When I came to the bottom of the trunk, I found the clothes I was wearing when I was found on the ledge on the riverbank.

"I thought you would want those," said Dr. Gilbert. "They are a part of your life."

I found myself weeping tears of joy, joy of knowing there were people so kind and loving and interested in me. Tears too of sadness, knowing that I must leave them. I threw my arms around each one and tried to thank them.

16
BACK ON THE RIVER

The next day Dr. Gilbert went to the steamboat office where he bought me a ticket on the *Virginia*. It was leaving for Pittsburgh on April 3. When he came home, he helped me write a letter to Dr. Locke to tell him when the boat would dock in Cincinnati.

The morning of April 3, Sweet Bell helped me pack my things, including my precious French marker. I went down to the parlor where Aunt Gertrude was working on her needlepoint. She reached behind her and handed me a little flat box as she said, "Littsie, I thought you would like this."

When I opened it, I found a needlepoint inside. On it was a picture of the Gilbert's house with the word "Welcome" sewn in bright yellow thread under it. "I'll treasure this always," I told her.

"Fold it carefully and put it in your bag," she smiled. Looking at the clock on the mantle she added, "Hurry along now, Littsie. You'll be late. The steamboat leaves at 5:00 o'clock. You don't have much time."

I threw my arms around Aunt Gertrude and hugged her.

"All right, Littsie, come now," she said, gently pushing me away. "When you travel to New Orleans again, you know you are always welcome in the Gilbert household."

Dr. Gilbert, Barbara, Kevin and I climbed into the carriage driven by Dan Powell and rode to the dock. As we got there, the steamboat's horn blew, signaling the passengers to come aboard. I hugged everyone and promised to write when I got to Cincinnati.

When I reached the main deck, the *Virginia's* horn sounded again. The crew pulled the gangplank on board and untied the ropes. Slowly the boat moved away from the dock. I put my things into my cabin and went to find Mrs. Malone.

Strolling down the deck toward the dining room, I heard her hearty laugh. I tiptoed into the room and called out, "Hello, Mrs. Malone." Startled to hear her name, she swung around.

"Good heavens, child!" she exclaimed, giving me a bear hug. Holding me at arms length she turned me around, admiring my new dress and said, "You look wonderful. You are a lovely young lady, Littsie."

"May I ask you for a favor, Mrs. Malone? I want to repay you for all you and the Captain did last November. Could I work for you on this trip to Cincinnati to pay back a little of all I owe you?"

"There is no need for that, child," replied Mrs. Malone. "But, I know you are a young woman of the Ohio country, with an independent mind and you will not change it. If you wish, we'll be happy to have you work for us on the *Virginia*," Mrs. Malone smiled. "Let me see, where is that girl? Maddie, come over here." Maddie strolled across the room looking as grumpy as she did when I first met her. "Maddie, you remember Littsie, don't you? She was with us last fall."

"Yes, ma'am, I guess I do," she said.

"We need someone to run errands and clear the tables for the waiters during meal time. Tomorrow morning before breakfast show Littsie what to do."

"Yes, Mrs. Malone, I'll do what I can," Maddie answered as she walked back across the room to finish setting the tables for dinner.

"My fine friend," said Mrs. Malone, "since the Captain and I want to hear all about New Orleans, have dinner with us at our table this evening. Tonight we will celebrate," she concluded, hugging me again.

The next day was warm and sunny. Once I finished my breakfast chores, I stood on the hurricane deck enjoying the ride on the river. A gentleman wearing a yellow and green plaid suit, a maroon high silk hat and carrying a walking stick, came up the stairs to join me. He took five long deep breaths and said, "Nothing like spring air on the river to clear the lungs!" Turning to me he continued, "Fine day for a journey up river, isn't it, miss, . . . miss," he stammered.

"Littsie O'Donnell," I answered, "and it is a fine day, sir."

"Pleased to meet you, Miss O'Donnell. My name is Dennis Grogan," he said, tipping his hat. "And where are you traveling, Miss O'Donnell?"

"I'm on my way to Cincinnati, sir."

"Ah, Porkopolis! Well, little lady, I've done a fair amount of business there. I'd have liked Cincinnati better if the citizens of that fair city did not love the raising and selling of hogs so much."

"Are the hogs still everywhere in Cincinnati, Mr. Grogan?"

"Yes, they are, little lady. The number of hogs in Cincinnati is not to be believed, unless you see it for yourself. Everyday the newspapers carry advertisements that read something like this: 'Wanted immediately 4,000 fat hogs!' or 'For sale, 2,000 barrels of prime pork!'" Mr. Grogan paused to catch his breath. As he headed down the stairs to the cabin deck, he added,

"Hope you enjoy your stay in Porkopolis! Best regards to
the hogs!"

My chores on the boat made each day pass quickly.
Still I thought of what might happen when I returned to
Cincinnati and couldn't find my sister, Megan. When the
Virginia passed Cairo, Illinois, I knew we would be in
Cincinnati in less than three days. But what went on in
those three days was more excitement than I ever care to
have again.

It was the next evening during dinner that a waiter
came racing into the dining room shouting, "A race is
on between the *Brandywine* and the *Hudson!* Come and
see!" Everyone in the dining room hurried out to the
rail to see the two steamboats race.

I was in the crowd at the rail, cheering the
steamboats as they raced down river. Huge sparks
sprayed out of the smoke stacks on both steamers.
Suddenly the *Hudson* lurched ahead. There was a
roaring explosion. Parts of the *Brandywine* flew into the
air. Flames raced over the decks of the *Brandywine* as
passengers jumped into the water to keep from being

burned alive. Everything was chaos! We heard the anguished cries of those still on the burning boat. We watched in horror as we saw people drown.

Captain Malone guided the *Virginia* closer to rescue those struggling to keep their heads above water. The crew threw them ropes. Some were pulled to safety. Others had the ropes tugged from their grasp by the river's swift current.

I ran down the stairs to the main deck, hoping to help those being lifted onto the boat. Suddenly I saw a tree in the water and a little black girl holding tight to it. I reached out as far as I could to grab hold of a branch so the child could drag herself on board.

The girl, who was about eight years-old, lay staring at me, shivering with cold, too frightened to talk. As one of the passengers ran down the main deck toward me, I jumped to my feet, grabbed the child's hand and dragged her behind the stairs.

After the person passed, cautiously, I took her to my cabin and led her inside.

When I saw she was wearing a heavy metal collar, I almost screamed aloud, "A slave! A child slave!" I decided no matter what happened she would not be anyone's slave again.

Opening my trunk, I gave her dry clothing. After she changed, she sat shivering on the edge of my bed, so I wrapped her in one of my blankets. She said her name was Euleen Randolph. Through chattering teeth, she told me what happened abroad the *Brandywine*.

She said the main deck was so packed with cargo, there was little room for the deck passengers. When the steamboat's boilers exploded, the scalding water and steam burst out, killing those hit by the blast. Other passengers were trapped, as the boat sank, because there was no way to escape.

"It was awful, just awful," Euleen cried, wiping tears from her eyes. "I was lucky I found a space between two bales of cotton, near the rail. When the boilers blew, I fell into the river. I would have drowned for sure if that tree hadn't been there for me to catch hold of," Euleen sighed.

"Were your parents with you?" I asked.

"No, missy," Euleen answered, "We were separated long ago. Master Jeremiah Meier was takin' me and the other slaves he bought at auction to his plantation just outside Richmond, Virginia. You gonna send me back to him, missy?"

"No, Euleen and please, don't call me 'Missy.' My name is Littsie O'Donnell. I'm going to Cincinnati and if I can get you on free soil in Ohio, I'll do just that."

"But, missy, I mean Miss Littsie, you can't," Euleen tried to interrupt.

"You stay right here, Euleen," I said, turning to leave the cabin. "I'll go to the kitchen and get you something to eat. Then we'll plan what to do."

Those rescued by the crew were being cared for in the dining room. I looked inside and searched each man's face trying to imagine which one was Mr. Jeremiah Meier. Had he been saved, I wondered.

On my way to the kitchen, I thought about Euleen. I knew I could hide her in my cabin by locking the door. Food would be easy. There were always leftovers from the serving tables. Since the *Virginia* was only a few days from Cincinnati, I felt sure no one would find her in that short time. But if I got caught, there would be trouble for the Malones and me. By law, slaves were a master's personal property. I had to be careful.

17
A SOLUTION

EULEEN slept on the couch that night, barely breathing. When I went to help with breakfast, I warned her not to make a sound. I would tell Maddie, before she cleaned the cabins, I had a little project and I would take care of my cabin. "Some project," I said, "she lives and breaths."

As I ran errands for the waiters, I listened to the talk about the race. Some of the passengers from the

Brandywine said the race started because the captains were young. They wanted to get into the steamer trade by winning a race. Others said the boats left the Evansville, Indiana, landing at the same time and this was a challenge to race.

"Whatever the reason," whispered a frail, gray haired woman, whose husband had drowned, "it turned into the most terrible tragedy."

When a big man said in a loud voice, "I'm lucky. I had seven slaves on the *Brandywine* and I've found all but one. She was about eight years-old and would have brought me a lot of money in a few years. A feisty one she was. I cannot believe she drowned." Turning to the crowd he announced, "I'll give five hundred dollars to have that little slave girl back."

"Five hundred dollars!" I whispered. Many on the *Virginia* would be willing to turn in a slave for that amount. When I got back to my cabin, I gave Euleen the few scrapes of bread and chicken and a small apple I saved for her. I told her about the reward. Since people were looking for her, Euleen's escape had to be perfect. Euleen showed me a plan we agreed just might work. She climbed into my steamer trunk and curled up inside. She said I could get a roustabout to carry it off the boat and no one would know she was inside.

"But, once the lid closes, you can't breathe!"

"Look, Miss Littsie," Euleen excitedly continued, "if we break the lock, we'll keep the trunk closed by tying a rope around it. We'll tie it loose, so I can push the trunk lid open to get air."

"It could work, Euleen," I said. "I'll get the rope and a hammer from the crew. We can easily break the lock." Fondly admiring my trunk I added, "the Gilberts gave me this beautiful trunk, I hate to damage it. But I know they would understand."

As I went below I heard two stewards whispering, "I wonder where that little black girl could be? Five hundred dollars!"

"Five hundred dollars, could buy me a little house and a few chickens. I'd be off this infernal steamboat!" the second man said.

Maddie ran toward me as I headed to my cabin with the hammer and the rope. She put her arm around my shoulders saying, "And how is your 'little project'? Can I come in to see it?"

"Of course, Maddie, before I leave the steamer. You can come in tomorrow," I stammered, backing away from her.

As I unlocked my cabin door and went inside, I whispered to Euleen, "Maddie suspects something, I just know she does. Your plan better work."

Taking the hammer I struck the lock with three powerful blows and it fell to the floor. Euleen climbed inside the trunk. As I tied a rope around it, she whispered, "If I knock three times, Miss Littsie, for Lord's sake, open the trunk, it means I can't breathe!"

Just as I finished tying the knot, Maddie pushed the door open and walked in saying, "Oh, Littsie, I heard some loud pounding in here. I thought you might need some help." Her eyes flashed around the room. She walked to the desk and asked, "What is this? Food in your cabin? Holding an apple core by the stem she said, "Is this my surprise?"

"No, Maddie. Here, I'll give you my 'little project.' It's a going away present." I chose a bright yellow dress, one the Gilberts gave me, and handed it to her, "Yellow will look beautiful on you, Maddie."

"Why, Littsie!" she exclaimed, "I'll try it on."

Thinking of Euleen, I said, "With all the mess in here, there's no room to change clothes. Take the dress and tell me at dinner if it fits."

As I gently steered her toward the cabin door, Maddie took one last look around the room. But she was so pleased with her new dress, she didn't even notice the trunk lid moving.

Once Maddie was gone, I closed my cabin door and locked it. Running to the trunk I whispered, "Euleen, are you all right?" Untying the rope I threw open the lid. Inside Euleen smiled up at me.

"It works!" she said in a loud whisper. "Miss Littsie, I could have stayed in here 'til the boat docks in Cincinnati tomorrow."

"You have a safe hiding place," I happily said, helping Euleen out of the trunk.

18
MEETING A TRUE FRIEND

*T*HE next morning at breakfast Maddie said as a going away gift she would let me stand at the buffet table to serve the guests, a duty she always kept for herself. But, if I ran errands for the waiters, I could watch my cabin door. Euleen was so close to freedom. Cincinnati was only hours away and I was afraid of being caught. After breakfast, when I got back to my cabin, Euleen was hiding in the trunk.

"I'm glad to see you, Miss Littsie," Euleen sighed. "Someone pushed and pushed at the cabin door. I'm glad you locked it," she smiled.

"It won't be long now, Euleen. When we get to Cincinnati, I'll take you to the Cincinnati Female Academy and at night you can escape," I whispered.

That afternoon, as I stood at the rail, we rounded a bend in the river. There she was, the Queen City, Cincinnati. Soon the familiar cobblestone landing, Main Street, and the neat little buildings that lined Water Street at the top of the landing came into view. Cincinnati was so small and quiet by comparison to New Orleans. Oh, how good it was to be home.

I looked up to the pilot house and seeing Captain Malone, waved to him and called out, "Good-bye and thank you." He smiled, tipped his hat, and called back "Good luck, Littsie!"

As I headed down the deck, Mrs. Malone saw me and smiled. She hugged me saying, "Dear Littsie, I pray you find your sister and you are safe in Cincinnati." Then she added, in a whisper, "When you are on the landing, trust the man who asks to carry your trunk."

I didn't understand Mrs. Malone. But there was no time to ask questions since the boat was docking. I ran to my cabin. When I got there the door was open and my trunk, carpetbag and Euleen were gone.

Maddie burst into my cabin laughing, "Ah, you look so worried, you poor little thing. Lost your luggage? Well, close your eyes and follow me," she laughed again.

Maddie led me to the deck rail. "Now, open your eyes and look down there!" she said gleefully. "I had the roustabouts take them for you. That was the least I could do to thank you for this lovely dress! Guess I should have told you, but I wanted it to be a surprise."

"Thank you, Maddie," I said, as I hurried down the stairs to the main deck, across the gangplank and on to the landing. When I got to my trunk, I knocked on it three times and heard a raspy voice say, "Arf! Arf!"

"Oh, Euleen, you're all right," I sighed with relief. Then a tall, strong looking black man tapped my shoulder saying, "Miss Littsie O'Donnell?"

"Yes," I replied, confused he knew my name.

"I am William Dobbins. A friend told us you needed someone to carry your trunk. May I help you?" he said, lifting my trunk onto his shoulder.

Picking up my carpetbag, I ran after him as he

headed toward a wagon. "I broke the lock on my trunk. Please be careful, Mr. Dobbins."

"Yes, Miss, yes, I can see that. I will be ever so careful with your trunk and everything in it."

As he slid the trunk into the back of the wagon, I said, "Mr. Dobbins, we, I mean I'm going to the Cincinnati Female Academy."

"Oh, no, Miss," he interrupted. "First we are going to see Mr. Nicholas Longworth. He lives just about two blocks away on Pike Street. Mr. Longworth knows a lot about fixing locks on trunks and the like. Believe me. Then you can go to the Cincinnati Female Academy."

He helped me into the seat next to him on the wagon and he took the reins as the horses pulled the wagon up the landing. We turned right and drove slowly down a long tree lined avenue.

"You will like Mr. Longworth, Miss O'Donnell," Dobbins confided. "He is a valuable friend. He always helps those in trouble." Saying this he shook the reins and the horses broke into a gallop. What would happen to me now? Would Nicholas Longworth help me? I never heard the man's name or saw his house. What would he do to me if he found Euleen? Then I remembered what Mrs. Malone said, "Trust the man who offers to help you with your trunk."

Dobbins guided the wagon into the driveway of a beautiful, white mansion surrounded by blooming dogwood trees. He stopped at the front door, helped me down from the wagon and lifted the trunk onto his shoulder. A young woman wearing a black dress and a crisply starched white apron appeared at the door. "I have some fixing for Mr. Longworth, Bess," Dobbins said, as we entered the front hall. The woman closed and bolted the door saying, "Wait, I'll tell Mr. Longworth, he is working in his garden."

A thin old gentleman with bushy brows and a long beak like nose ran down the hallway from the back of the house. His mouth turned down at the corners as though he spent most of his life dissatisfied with what he saw. The sleeves of his white shirt were rolled above his elbows and his black trousers and boots were splattered with mud. When he looked at me, his steel blue eyes cut straight through to the truth.

"Who is this young lady, Mr. Dobbins?"
"First we have Miss Littsie O'Donnell and then we

have her trunk," Dobbins replied.

"And what is so special about this?" he asked, as he untied the rope and opened the trunk. Euleen was curled up inside.

"What is your name, little one?" Mr. Longworth kindly asked.

"Euleen, sir, Euleen Randolph."

"Euleen Randolph," Mr. Longworth repeated in a gentle voice. "I'm sure you've been in this trunk so long you cannot stand. Bring me that wooden chair, Dobbins. Bess, can you get the blacksmith?"

"No, Mr. Longworth!" I protested. "Are you sending for the sheriff to take us to jail?"

Mr. Longworth laughed, "Oh, no," and before he explained, he started laughing again. Then he said, "You are brave, but foolish girls. You know that, don't you?" Neither one of us could look at him. "Let me assure you," he continued, "no one in my house, nor the German blacksmith I sent for, will harm you. The blacksmith must remove this vile collar from Euleen's neck."

Suddenly a young man about twenty years-old, with black curly hair burst into the hall shouting, "Father, a man is coming down Fourth Street at full gallop headed for our house."

"Joseph, get Salmon Chase. Tell him to come here with five hundred dollars and the papers I'll need to buy a slave," Longworth demanded.

Bess hurried Euleen off to the back of the house.

Dobbins unbolted the front door, went out and drove the wagon away. Then Mr. Longworth pushed the trunk into the hall closet.

"Now, young lady," Longworth said, as he buttoned his shirt sleeves and put on a black frock coat, "let me handle everything."

We heard the sound of galloping horses on the gravel driveway in front of the Longworth mansion. There was a loud knocking on the door. Longworth opened it as if he were expecting someone to pay a friendly visit. As he did, Mr. Jeremiah Meier strode into the room.

"Good afternoon, sir, and what do I owe the honor of this visit?" Longworth smiled.

"My name is Jeremiah Meier, Mr. Longworth. I understand you have some of my property."

"What makes you think . . ." Mr. Longworth began to ask.

Mr. Meier continued, "You are hiding my slave, Euleen Randolph, Mr. Longworth. This is against the law. As a gentleman, you know that."

"Yes, sir, I am fully aware of that fact. If I do have the little girl, how much is she worth?"

"She is not for sale, Mr. Longworth."

"Oh, Mr. Meier, everything has a price," replied Mr. Longworth. "What do you want with her? She is a wiry little devil. She'll only run away again and you'll have to pay to get her back. She is lame now too and could hardly stand when she came in here."

"So you admit it, Mr. Longworth. Where is she? I demand you return her to me!"

"I never denied she was here," said Mr. Longworth. "I asked what you wanted for a lame, incorrigible runaway. Think about it, Mr. Meier."

"Well, sir, if I kept her for four years, I could easily get five hundred dollars," replied Mr. Meier.

"That's if she doesn't run away in those four years, Mr. Meier. I'll tell you what I'll do. I will give you five hundred dollars right now to save you those four years of frustration."

"You are not making fun of me, are you?"

"No, no, Mr. Meier, nothing of the sort."

"Let me see your money then, Longworth. I'll not leave here until I have the cash in my hand."

"I sent my son, Joseph, for the money and a lawyer, Mr. Salmon Chase," assured Mr. Longworth. "Of course, it is illegal to buy or sell slaves in Ohio. For your five hundred dollars, I hope you will take a short voyage on the ferry across the Ohio River to Kentucky. There Mr. Chase will finish this business and you will have your money, Mr. Meier."

"That's agreeable to me."

"Step this way. Perhaps you would like a glass of wine while we wait for Mr. Chase," Longworth said, leading Mr. Meier into the parlor.

How easily they bought and sold a human life. What would become of Euleen now? Had I saved her from one master only to serve another?

There was a knock at the front door and Bess welcomed the visitor. In one hand he carried a small metal box, in the other he clutched some papers. Bess led him into the parlor.

"Meet Mr. Jeremiah Meier of Richmond, Virginia, Mr. Chase. He wants five hundred dollars for his slave child," said Mr. Longworth.

Mr. Chase counted the money on the parlor table. "Mr. Meier, I'm sure Nicholas has explained, that Ohio is a free state. This money cannot change hands here. If you will join me," he said, replacing the money in the metal box, "we'll go to Kentucky where you can sign this deed giving ownership to Mr. Longworth of . . . "

. . . "Miss Euleen Randolph," Mr. Longworth replied, as Mr. Chase wrote Euleen's name on two pieces of paper.

"In return I will give you the five hundred dollars," Mr. Chase concluded. Mr. Longworth signed both papers where Chase had written Euleen's name. Then Mr. Meier signed them and left one on the table.

"I hadn't planned a journey to Kentucky. But it's worth the trip to get five hundred dollars for a lame

MEETING A TRUE FRIEND

slave child!" he laughed heartily. "It's a pleasure doing business with you, Mr. Longworth. If you are ever in Richmond, please come and see me. Perhaps we can do business again," he smiled, shaking Longworth's hand. Then he followed Mr. Chase.

Longworth closed the door behind them as I ran toward him, crying, "Euleen will not be your slave! I will find a way to stop you!"

Longworth grabbed my hands and held them. I sank to my knees weeping at the thought of what would become of Euleen. He went into the parlor and returned with the paper Mr. Chase left. Handing it to me he asked, "Can you read this to me?"

Wiping the tears from my eyes, I took the paper and read:

"'*Know all men by this document that I, Nicholas Longworth, of Ohio, County of Hamilton, do for divers good cause and reason to me well known, do manumit, enfranchise and set at liberty the Negro child, Euleen Randolph.*'

Oh, Mr. Longworth," I shouted, "this means Euleen is free!"

"Meier had to think I wanted a slave," Longworth explained. "He would not sell Euleen if he knew I would free her. People like Mr. Jeremiah Meier demand playacting. Now there is someone in the kitchen much more interested in this paper than we are, Miss O'Donnell."

"Let her read it," I told Mr. Longworth. Sadly

Euleen said she couldn't read, write or do her numbers. Slaves were not allowed to book learn.

"Oh, Euleen, this paper sets you free!" I cried.

Euleen looked at Mr. Longworth and asked, "Is it true, sir?"

"Yes, you are free to do what you wish."

I handed the paper to Euleen and she sat staring at it in disbelief. "Oh, Mr. Longworth, thank you," she sobbed, "but I have no kin folk and no where to go."

"Euleen, would you work here as Bess's helper? You would have your own room. The work will not be hard and I will pay you for your labor."

"That sounds wonderful, Mr. Longworth," Euleen smiled.

19
ONLY A SINGLE CLUE

*W*ITH the excitement of getting Euleen to safety, I forgot about all of my own problems. As Dobbins drove me on his wagon to the Cincinnati Female Academy, I looked into the face of every child I saw, hoping to see Megan. When we arrived at the school, Dobbins carried my trunk up the steps to the front door where I pulled the bell chain. There were footsteps on the hard wooden floor inside. A man wearing a dark green coat opened the door and said, "I am Dr. John Locke, may I help you?"

Opening my bag, I took the letter he sent and handed it to him. Dr. Locke smiled as he said, "Ah, Littsie, we've been expecting you." Dobbins carried my trunk into the hall.

"I hope you will come to visit Mr. Longworth, Euleen, Bess and me," he smiled.

"Of course I will, Dobbins," I called after him as he headed back to his wagon.

Dr. Locke asked me to follow him down a long wood paneled hallway to his office. He went behind his desk and told me to sit in the chair opposite him.

"Littsie, you will work at the Academy to pay for your classes and your board. Some of your chores will be to dust the floors everyday and wax them once a week. Also, you will work in the kitchen and do whatever Mrs. Craymore, the cook, asks. You'll wash the dishes, set the tables for each meal and go to the market every morning to do the day's shopping. The students who board at the Academy live in the dormitory on the second floor. The cook and housekeeper and her helpers share a room on the third floor. Do you have any questions, Littsie?"

"Where are the classrooms, Dr. Locke?"

"In the two large parlors behind my office."

"And where will I take my meals, sir?"

"The kitchen and dining room are downstairs. Once you finish serving the students their food, you will eat in the kitchen with Mrs. Craymore, the cook and housekeeper, and Patricia Casper, another student who works to pay her room and board."

Looking again at my letter he continued, "You said you do not know what became of your sister."

"Yes, I want to begin searching for her as soon as possible. Perhaps she is here in Cincinnati."

"Cincinnati is a large city of over 26,000 people, Littsie. You cannot wander the streets alone. I know you want to find her. But you may only go out if you have a place to look for her. Do you understand?"

"Yes, Dr. Locke, I do."

"I asked Patricia Casper to show you around and introduce you to the others who work at the school," Dr. Locke added, pulling a long cord hanging by the window that made a bell ring in another room. After a few minutes, the large oak door leading to the school's main hall opened and in walked a girl my age. She wore a dark blue dress and had pink ribbons tied to the ends of her braided hair. "I'm Patricia Casper, Littsie. Dr. Locke told me all about you. First, I'll show you our room and then we'll go down to supper," Patricia said.

"I'll have Howard, the caretaker, bring your trunk to your room, Littsie," Dr. Locke smiled, as Patricia led me out of the room.

Half way up the stairs I suddenly remembered my manners. Turning, I ran back, sliding on the well polished wooden floors and knocked on the door that led to Dr. Locke's office. I thanked him for giving me a place to live and work to earn my keep and go to school.

"You're welcome, Littsie. Run along now," he said,

as I closed the door and joined Patricia, who was waiting for me on the stairs.

"Our room is small but cozy," Patricia smiled. Over there we study our lessons," she said, pointing to a small table with two wooden straight-backed chairs on either side. "That's Mrs. Craymore's bed on the far side of the room. This is mine by the door. You can have one of those two beds, over there."

Looking out the open window she said, "From here you can see the hills that surround Cincinnati and down there is the Ohio River. The sunsets are the best." A gentle breeze billowed the sheer white drapes at the window. Taking a deep breath, she continued, "Sometimes at night you can smell the river when the breeze blows in like that. Come on, Littsie. Mrs. Craymore will wonder what happened to us. She made a special soda bread for supper to welcome you." Taking my hand, she led me to the kitchen.

The next morning at my school desk I found a new copybook, a quill pen and a bottle of ink. Patricia whispered, "You can thank Dr. Locke, Littsie. I saw him put them there for you."

After our classes, Patricia and I waxed the floors together. As we worked, we talked about Megan and how to find her. When I asked Patricia what she would do, she said, "If she were my sister, I'd put an ad in the newspaper." So that's what I did and I used the money Dr. Gilbert gave me for my journey, to pay for it.

This is what I had printed in the Cincinnati Gazette:

THE CINCINNATI GAZETTE

LOST CHILD - MEGAN O'DONNELL, RED HAIR, FIVE YEARS-OLD. MEGAN DISAPPEARED FROM THE O'DONNELL CABIN IN COLUMBIA, OHIO, OCTOBER 24, 1832, DURING THE CHOLERA EPIDEMIC. ANYONE KNOWING HER WHEREABOUTS, PLEASE CONTACT MISS LITTSIE O'DONNELL, CINCINNATI FEMALE ACADEMY, FOURTH AND WALNUT STREET, CINCINNATI, OHIO.

Each day after the ad was in the paper, we waited for some news. But there was no reply. Then one day Patricia burst into our room saying, "Littsie, this should make you happy, I think I have a lead. A new girl came to the school with her parents to meet with Dr. Locke. I was outside his office dusting the floors and heard them speaking. They asked where they should have their noon meal and Dr. Locke said, 'The Apencer House has the finest food in the whole Ohio country.' And, Littsie, he said a lot of important people go there. I bet someone will know where you should look for your sister."

"It's worth a try," I said.

I asked Dr. Locke if I could go to the Apencer House to see if anyone knew what became of children during the cholera epidemic. He agreed I could go when my chores were finished. "Just to the Apencer

House then back to the Academy," he said.

The Apencer House was a two-story stone building on Water Street, facing the public landing. I climbed the three steps to the door of the restaurant. As I entered, a waiter called to me saying, "You are too late for lunch little girl. Come back with your parents for dinner."

"But, sir . . . " I tried to protest.

"Be off with you, child, no customers after 2:00 o'clock," he insisted, closing the door.

I started down the steps, as the waiter opened the door for two customers saying, "Both of you are always the last to leave. See you again tomorrow." He closed and locked the door behind them.

One of them said to the other as they headed down the landing, "Yes, of course I know him, Dr. Drake is one of the best doctors in the Ohio country."

"Dr. Drake!" I whispered aloud. "He will know!"

I ran up Main Street to the Cholera Hospital. As I did, all my memories of October rushed through my head. I remember the people, the buildings and how Papa and Mama died. But when I got to the place where the hospital had been, it wasn't there. Breathlessly I asked a man, "Sir, begging your pardon, where is the hospital that was here last fall?"

"Oh, that is not a hospital, miss. It is the Cincinnati Medical College. The hospital is the big gray building on Sixth Street."

When I reached the hospital, I ran up the front steps and into the lobby. I asked a woman carrying a large tray filled with blue colored medicine bottles, "Where can I find Dr. Drake?"

"He sees patients this afternoon in his office on Vine Street."

"Please, ma'am," I insisted, as she turned to go down the hall, "Where is his office?"

"You'll see the house. It's the large red brick one in the middle of the block. It has white columns on the porch that reach to the roof. There is a sign with Dr. Drake's name on it in the window. The front door will be open. You can go right inside."

"Thank you, ma'am, thank you," I called over my shoulder as I fled down the steps and headed toward Dr. Drake's.

Many of the houses that lined Vine Street were built with red brick, but only one had tall white columns. As I dashed up the walk to the front door, I saw the small hand painted sign in the window that read, "Dr. Drake's Clinic."

The waiting room was filled with people. I sat in a chair by the door. A medical aide came over to me and asked what sickness I thought I had. I told him I was not sick but I had to see Dr. Drake as soon as possible. Since I was so out of breath from running and looked so pale, I'm sure he thought the doctor should see me immediately. He led me into a small examination room.

A few minutes later, Dr. Drake walked in brushing his thick auburn hair from his forehead. He stared at me with his clear blue-eyes and asked, "Well, young lady, what seems to be the problem?" Sitting down on a white straight-backed chair across from me, he waited for my answer.

"Dr. Drake, I know you don't remember me, but I'm Littsie O'Donnell from Columbia, Ohio. Back in October, you gave me medicine for my Papa when he was sick with cholera." Then I told him about the death of my parents and my search for Megan.

Dr. Drake listened thoughtfully and when I finished, he said, "There is a slim chance, she was taken to the Orphan Asylum, near Baymiller Street at the west end of the city. The truth is, so many children were left on their own during the cholera epidemic, she may be someplace else. I would take you there, but I am leaving this evening for St. Louis. Perhaps Dr. Locke can help you," he suggested.

"I'll walk to the Orphan Asylum by myself," I vowed, happily shaking his hand, hopeful that I would find Megan.

Dr. Drake smiled and putting his arm around my shoulders, led me to the door saying, "Good luck, Miss Littsie O'Donnell. I will return from St. Louis in two weeks. If you do not find your sister by then, please me again and I will try to help you."

There was a beautiful pink haze in the late afternoon sky. The golden sun shone in the windows of the elegant homes as I ran along Vine Street back to the Academy. I knew Dr. Locke could punish me for not returning to the Academy when I left the Apencer House, but I had to see Dr. Drake, I just had to.

2⊙
A FATE DECIDED

*W*HEN she saw me, Patricia called from our bedroom window, "Look, Littsie, a letter from your friend, Anne Bell Bailey!"

"She's alive!" I shouted joyfully. I ran up the stairs to our room. When Patricia handed me the letter, I stood staring at the envelope. I was afraid of the news inside. I sat on my bed and slowly, cautiously, opened it and began to read aloud:

May 15, 1833
Dear Littsie,

I couldn't believe my eyes when I saw your ad in the Cincinnati Gazette.

First, let me tell you all I know about your sister. On that day back in October, I came by your folks' house in the afternoon. Your Papa was doing poorly and I knew he wasn't going to make it. I looked at your Mama and I knew she had only a few hours left in her too.

I asked her where you might be and she said she sent you to Cincinnati. I couldn't get anything else out of her and I took it you were safe with friends there.

I swept little Megan up in my arms and was about to take her with me when she set up an awful fuss. She wanted to bring the French marker, the one you found on the Ohio River bank. She was playing with the marker when I came into the cabin. I brought it with us to get her to settle down.

We doubled back to the cave. Halfway there, I saw Alana following us at a distance. I called to her and she came running, so she joined us too. When I got to the cave, I put out the fire, threw the covers over the bed real fast and we left for Gallipolis.

On our way, my horse went lame on the rugged trail I took as a short cut. By this time, I had a touch of the cholera myself, but I lay in the path all night, holding tight to Megan. Luckily, early the next day, a farmer found us and took us to his place.

*I got so sick with cholera, they didn't think I'd make it.
Thank heavens the farmer's wife kept nursing me! They
were older folks and since they were taking care of me they
couldn't take care of Megan at the same time. A family
with seven children stopped at the farm one afternoon
and the couple asked if they would take Megan. They
agreed to care for her and said they were heading for
Cincinnati. Though the cholera was so bad there, I doubt
they made that their destination. What I'm trying to say,
Littsie, is I have no idea of what became of your little
Megan.*

I almost fainted when I read this. I struggled to see the
words on the page:

*When I was well enough to travel, Alana and I made our
way to my son's home in Gallipolis where I stayed for a
few weeks to regain my strength. Since I still wasn't well,
my son sent me home, knowing I'd get a good rest there.*

*Alana is with William in Gallipolis. In his letters he says
she is just fine. When you have a place to keep her, you
can have her back.*

*My plan is to be in Cincinnati by June. I'll keep my eyes
peeled for you when I get there. I might stay at the St.
George Guest House or the Sign of the Blue Tailed
Monkey or the Cincinnati Hotel. I'm not sure which one*

will let an ol' polecat like me in any of them fine places.

Sorry I can't give you better news about Megan. Hope to see you soon in Cincinnati.

Your friend,
Anne Bell Bailey

"How will you find Megan now?" Patricia sighed.

"This afternoon Dr. Drake told me about a place where they put homeless children from the cholera epidemic. I'm going to ask Dr. Locke's permission to go there tomorrow."

"Oh, Dr. Locke! He asked everyone where you were and he said as soon as you got back he wants to see you in his office immediately."

I knocked ever so softly on the door to Dr. Locke's office. Walking in, I stood before him and said, "Sir, I received this letter today from my friend, a woman named Anne Bell Bailey, who lived in Columbia, Ohio. I want you to read it."

Dr. Locke read the letter and smiled happily saying, "This is wonderful news, Littsie! Perhaps Megan is alive and here in Cincinnati!" Then changing his tone of voice, he continued, "Littsie, this letter does not explain your whereabouts this afternoon, when you left the Apencer House."

I told him about Dr. Drake and begged his permission to go to the Orphan Asylum the next day.

"No, I'm afraid that will not be possible, Littsie.
That is in a lonely part of the city. Howard has too much
to do right now. Perhaps sometime next week he can
take you there."

"Next week!" I cried.

"I know how anxious you are to find your sister, but
it seems not even Dr. Drake holds out much hope of
finding her at the Asylum. I cannot have Howard taking
time from his work to drive you around the city. Next
week will be soon enough."

"Yes, sir," I said, choking back my tears.

"Don't you think Mrs. Craymore needs you in the
kitchen to help with supper, Littsie?"

"Yes, Dr. Locke," I said, leaving his office.

The next day was one of the students, Lila
Timmerman's, birthday. A special dinner was to be
prepared in her honor. It was barely daylight when the
three of us, Mrs. Craymore, Patricia and I, left the
Academy and headed for the market. Mrs. Craymore
went from stall to stall examining the fruits, vegetables
and meats, selecting only the very best for the birthday
meal.

As we started back to the Academy, we saw a crowd
gathered in front of the St. George Guest House.
Someone in the midst of the group was shouting at a
man who stood at the door with his hands on his hips.

"I've eaten ten day-old rattlesnake that tasted better
than the grub you serve," a woman shouted.

"I'm sorry, ma'am . . . " the waiter tried to say.

"Why you should be sorry!" the woman shouted. "Cook that dragon on your sign for dinner! It'll be more tasty than that greasy boot leather you tried to pass off as bacon this morning! Good day to you, sir!" she shouted as she turned and headed down the street toward us. Then she saw me.

"Anne Bell Bailey!" I cried.

"Littsie O'Donnell! Well, ain't you a sight for sore eyes!" she cried, as she ran toward me and caught me up in her arms.

"Your letter arrived yesterday!" I told her.

"Well, then, it's fate we're here together," Anne Bell laughed. "I just arrived in town. I was going to stop by the Cincinnati Female Academy this very day to see you. I thought you might want to head out to your land to see how things are. I'm going to Columbia this afternoon. Want to come along?"

"I wish I could, Anne Bell," I sighed. But I . . ." Suddenly I remembered Mrs. Craymore and Patricia. They just stared in amazement at the two of us. I introduced them and then asked Anne Bell for a very special favor. "If the principal of the Academy will allow it, will you drive me this afternoon to the Orphan Asylum to see if Megan is there?"

"Of course, child," she responded. "Although I don't know where it is, I'll ask around and find out. When do you want me to stop by to get you?"

"Not until after 2:00 o'clock, when my lunch chores are finished."

"I'll be in my wagon in front of the Academy at 2:00 o'clock this afternoon."

"Come along, Littsie. Dr. Locke will not let you go with Miss Bailey if you are late for your classes," Mrs. Craymore said, as we started up the street.

Just before lunch I met Dr. Locke in the hall and told him how lucky I was to meet Anne Bell Bailey. I pleaded with him to let me go with her and promised only to go to the Orphan Asylum and no other place. Perhaps because I sounded so desperate, he could hardly refuse, cautioning me, "You may go, but remember, no side trips!"

"Yes, sir, Dr. Locke, thank you, Dr. Locke!" I called running to tell Patricia and Mrs. Craymore.

It was a sunny day, but the air was cool. Mrs. Craymore told me to wear my cape and a bonnet. I took them from the closet and then pulled out my steamer trunk, raised the lid, and reached down into the bottom for the French marker. As I put it in my shoulder bag, I said, "Perhaps this will bring me luck!"

"For your sake, Littsie, I hope it will," Patricia said, walking into the room. "I hope you find your sister," Patricia called after me, as I headed down the stairs. Anne Bell helped me up to the seat on the wagon next to her and we drove off down Walnut Street.

"A man at the livery stable said the Orphan Asylum is in the Mill Creek bottoms, about a quarter of a mile north of the Plank Road. We have a long ride ahead of us, my girl," Anne Bell said, as she guided the horses into spacious tree lined Fifth Street.

"What if Megan isn't in the Orphan Asylum?"

"Hush, child! Don't say such a thing," she responded, refusing to admit this possibility.

"But," I continued, "what if she isn't there? What if she is still with the family? Or what if she is dead?"

"I can't answer those questions, Littsie," Anne Bell replied, gently putting her arm around my shoulders. We rode together in silence for a long while. Then I remembered the Kerry poem. I began whispering it to myself.

"Speak up, child," Anne Bell insisted. "I can't hear you."

"It's a poem my father learned as a child in Dingle, County Kerry, and he taught it to me. When he was troubled, he said it because the poem gave him a feeling of peace. This is how it goes:

I am the air that kisses the waves,
I am the wave of the deep,
I am the whisper of the surf,
I am the eagle on the cliff,
I am a ray from the pure sun,
I am the grace of growing things,
I am a lake in the rolling meadow,
Who if not I."

"And do you believe the eagle on the cliff will protect you, my dear Littsie?"

"I don't know, Anne Bell, perhaps today we'll learn the answer."

"The man at the stable told me we take a right turn here on Mound Street," Anne Bell said, seeing a sign on a wooden post. "Then we take a left on a narrow roadway that leads toward the Mill Creek. Since he never comes this way, he says from that point on, we're on our own."

We headed toward the western edge of the city, through the broad Mill Creek Valley, where few houses lined the sides of the roads. As the wagon lurched and jogged from side to side, Anne Bell struggled with the horses to keep them on the muddy, rugged roadway.

"I'm afraid of breaking a wheel on this old wagon of mine, Littsie. We'll have to leave it here and walk the rest of the way," Anne Bell said, pulling the horses reins and jumping down from the wagon.

Seeing a man ahead on the road, Anne Bell called out, "Hello there, sir! Wait up for us!" The man turned as we ran toward him.

"Sir, where is the Cincinnati Orphan Asylum?" Anne Bell asked.

"It's up over the hill. I'm headin' in that direction, you can walk along with me if you like."

"The spring rain made a mess of these roads. This here is called the lowlands of Mill Creek," he told us. "Not many folks come out this way. No reason to," he added. "We'll climb over this fence, a short cut I always take. Here, miss, let me give you a hand," he said, as he helped me over the fence rails.

"Watch the mud, Littsie. Try to walk on the grass where you can get a foothold," Anne Bell advised.

"This ground is so soggy," I said struggling to keep from getting my feet caught in the oozing mud.

Everywhere there were large pools of green, stagnant water. The three of us trudged through the wet fields, climbing over more split rail fences. Finally, in the distance, we saw a small, wretched building in the middle of an old cemetery.

"You can see the Orphan Asylum from here, it is just ahead."

"That can't be it!" I gasped.

"Why is that, little lady?" the man asked.

"I thought the building and grounds would be like the Cincinnati Female Academy," I replied.

"Not at all, miss. Nothing so grand for these poor children. The Asylum is in the middle of a paupers' cemetery. The house the children are living in was once the caretaker's. He died years ago. Seems if more than ten people were living in that house it would be cramped. But I hear as many as thirty children are there now and more arriving everyday," the man said.

"Does anyone take care of the children?"

"A woman named Miss Tribby does her best. She's the manager. I spoke to her once. Says she is barely able to feed them a small roll and milk for breakfast, a bowl of soup for lunch and a slice of dark bread and a dish of beans for dinner. She gives them what motherly care she can. Well, I turn off here. Good day, ladies," the man said, as he went down the road.

"Those must be the orphans playing off there in the fields. Look at their clothes, all ragged and dirty," I said. "If we find Megan in that crowd and she is well, it will be a miracle, Anne Bell."

A tall thin woman stood on the front porch watching us as we approached. She wore a dark brown dress. Drying her hands on the dirty white apron tied around her waist, she called out, "Hello, there, I'm Miss Tribby, manager of this Orphan Asylum. Why are you poking around here?"

"My name is Anne Bell Bailey and this is Miss Littsie O'Donnell. She is looking for her sister, a child named Megan, who may have been brought here during the cholera epidemic."

"I see," Miss Tribby said, smiling kindly at me and then frowning, "Now what was the child's name?"

"Megan, Megan O'Donnell," I said softly.

Miss Tribby responded, "We have no Megan O'Donnell here. I am sorry, child."

When she said this, I felt as dizzy

as that terrible afternoon in Columbia when I realized Megan was gone. I clutched the French marker in my bag and whispered to myself, "Megan is here, she must be here!"

"Perhaps Megan couldn't pronounce her name just right when she was brought here. I mean, maybe you misunderstood her. She is a little red haired four . . . no, five year-old with a beautiful Irish smile."

"I'm afraid there are lots of redheads here with beautiful Irish smiles," Miss Tribby sadly replied. "I suppose you could be right about mistaking her name. You can walk around and look at the children, but don't talk to them. They feel every stranger who comes here will adopt them."

Slowly I walked toward one group of children playing at the end of the porch. Carefully I looked at each one's face. None of them was at all like Megan. Out under a clump of trees were other groups. As I walked toward them, I passed an old water barrel. When I heard the song a tiny voice was singing nearby, I stood still. It was a song our family often sang.

> *The boatman dance and the boatman sing,*
> *The boatman is up to everything.*
> *Hi-ho, away we go,*
> *Floating down the river on the O-hi-o.*

I moved close enough to the child to look at her face without her seeing me. She kept singing, turning her little red head in time with the music. As I saw the child's face, I felt a burst of joy. She looked just like Megan! But was it Megan? The child's hair was cut short and her clothing was torn and dirty. Still I wanted to take the child into my arms and hug her. I dashed back to the porch where Miss Tribby and Anne Bell were standing and feeling faint stammered, "I believe I found Megan! But, how can I be sure?"

"Which one do you think is Megan?" Miss Tribby asked, looking at the groups of children in the fields.

"Over there, near the old rain barrel. She is singing a song about the boatman on the river. My family often sang that song."

"We are a river town, Littsie. Many people in Cincinnati sing that song," sighed Miss Tribby. "Is there any other way you can identify her?"

"Perhaps there is one way," I said, as I carefully took the French marker from my bag and showed it to Miss Tribby. "My sister, Megan, carried the other half of this marker with her when she and Anne Bell left Columbia in October."

Miss Tribby took the marker from me in disbelief. "Why, yes," she stammered, "Mary carried something like this with her when a neighbor found her wandering alone on the far road. She would not give it up and to this day, it is in the children's room on the windowsill."

"Then that little girl could be my sister, Megan. Please, Miss Tribby, I waited so long to hold her. Please, ma'am," I begged.

"All right, child, but gently. We don't want to frighten her. Go to her gently."

Cautiously, I approached the child still singing the boatman's song. I began singing the words to the song with her, "The boatman dance, the boatman sing," Megan turned to see who was singing the song.

"It's me, Megan! Littsie! I'm here to take you home," I cried. The child hesitated, frowned, smiled, then laughed and jumped into my open arms, knocking me to the ground.

"Littsie, where have you been? I looked all over for you. I didn't know where you went," she cried, tears streaming down her face.

"I've been searching for you, praying that someday I would find you. Oh, my little Megan, my beautiful little Megan," I said, hugging her. Taking her hand, I pointed to the porch steps saying, "Look who brought me to you, Megan."

"Anne Bell!" Megan shouted.

"Megan, my darlin'," Anne Bell laughed, sweeping Megan up in her arms and swinging her in the air. "Will you come along with us?" she asked.

"Oh, yes!" Megan happily said, "but wait a minute. I must get something." She ran up the porch steps and into the house. When she returned, she carried the other half of the French marker. Handing it to me, we joined the two halves together as I joyfully proclaimed, "This is Megan, my sister!"

The three of us rode back to town laughing and singing. When we came to the Academy, Anne Bell helped Megan and me down from the wagon.

"Well, Anne Bell, I don't know how to thank you! This is not good-bye, though," I smiled, hugging her.

"No, not by a long shot. I'll stop to visit as often as I can. When I'm in Columbia tomorrow, I'll see that your house and land are all right. Whenever you want to go to Columbia, let me know."

"Thank you, Anne Bell," we smiled, holding tight to each other's hand.

That evening, Dr. Locke declared the dinner a double celebration. First, the happy birthday of Lila Timmerman and a special welcome for little Megan O'Donnell. The students agreed it was a wonderful party, especially for the O'Donnell sisters.

Long after Mrs. Craymore and Patricia had fallen asleep, Megan and I told each other where we had been and what happened to us while we were separated. When Megan asked about our Papa and Mama, I told her, as gently as I could, that both of them died of cholera and were safe now in heaven. Hugging Megan, I whispered, "It will be a struggle for us, my little one, but everything will be all right. I just know it. I believe it for a fact."

I tucked Megan into the bed next to mine. I felt so peaceful now that I found her. We were together, a family again. I looked at the marker and put it on the shelf above our beds.

A gentle breeze billowed the curtains at the window. Off in the distance there was a steamboat's horn echoing against the soft rising hills. Such a beautiful sound, I thought, and soon I was asleep.

"What happened after that, Grandma?" Annie asked. Did you and your sister go back to your farm?"

Oh, Annie, that was another adventure. I'll need a month of snowy days to tell you the story about our farm and how Dr. Drake helped me. Look, children, the snow has stopped and the sun is coming out. Run! Get your sleds, go along outside and enjoy yourselves. There will be other days for more of my tales from long ago.

THE END